Teuflehund

Teuflehund

A novel

Rick Loughran (RiLo)

Order this book online at www.trafford.com
or email orders@trafford.com

Most Trafford titles are also available at major online book retailers.

Printed in the United States of America.

ISBN: 978-1-4269-2985-4 (sc)
ISBN: 978-1-4269-2986-1 (e)

Trafford rev. 12/15/2010

 www.trafford.com

North America & International
toll-free: 1 888 232 4444 (USA & Canada)
phone: 250 383 6864 ♦ fax: 812 355 4082

CONTENTS

FOREWARD

South America

It was the dark just before the dawn in Chinantla, a village located in the Uxpanapa Valley. It was one of many poblados filled with Chinanteco, Zoque and Totonaco people. Little Marcos sat dutifully on the wooden bench in the little room behind the altar of the church. When he slipped in he saw all the candles burning on the right reflecting a beam of light off the figure of Christ on the Cross at the rear of the church. They were lit in prayers to Padre Jesus of Chinantla that purveyor of miracles. Five year old Marcos would like a miracle, he would like the priest to go away and never come back, but that would not be.

He could hear the priests car rumbling up the steep hill to the blue church with the figure of Padre Jesus which had been decked with $50 bill, expired immigration document even gold bracelets asking for blessings for this was festival day. In an hour a procession of old women in shawls and toothless men would file up the hill to sing a birthday song to Padre Jesus.

It would not be long before the priest came into the room. There would be the honey of course, that was always nice, but to lick it from the priest as he was told to do seemed more wrong each time. It always felt good when he was fondled and kissed but when he had to bend over it cancelled that small pleasure He had tried to tell his mother and father but was quickly punished for lying and sent to bed with not even one tortilla.

Resentment for all humanity was building up in his young psyche, resentment that would know no borders and would erupt often and viciously. This young lump of Mexican clay was being formed into what would one day take a set of a serial molester himself accompanied by an ability to take life with the same abandon he was forced to take this sexual abuse.

North America

Little Michael, Mikey they called him, had been through a lot for a two year old boy. His father had left and his mother left him with others quite often so as to work. Life was not through pummeling this boy as it took his mother in a drunken accident of a holiday meant for joy and loving.

He felt longing for this forbidden woman, a longing she had created by judiciously tempering their relationship with innuendo and casual, seemingly innocent, displays of her full, sensuous body. His teen-aged world would not be like others; filled with sock hops, ice cream socials and baseball games. It would be one of warm thighs and breasts offset by hard work. His would be a world of compassionate detachment by a stepfather he loved and his common-law wife who loved young boys.

He had gotten into her bed as she suggested and lay their filled with sexual longing and guilt for that longing. It was dark in the bedroom but her heard her enter quietly, smelled her perfume and suddenly she was in beside him, a large breasted thirty years old nymphomaniac about to satisfied an as yet undefined hunger and need for the endorphins she would release as she took him into her warm arms and pressed his face into her generous breasts. This was just the start.

An Epiphany

It was a debutante day, cheerful and bright. The zephyr created by the warming of dawn wafted the sweet scent of lilacs into the room. The prelude to the opera "Delibes Lakme" flowed out of the stereo speakers.

An oboe mourned the passing of the night harmonizing with the soft moans emanating from the bed as the rising sun cast a faint cherry-pink hue on the bedroom wall. The melody and the sun rose in subdued elegance. Morning and life were here. Their bodies had emulated the elegant harmony of the two sopranos rising and falling passionately. Rita had stayed the night, something she had not done before. Her head rested on his arm and her large, firm breasts rested against his chest. Not very tall, about five feet, she had the smooth, olive skin denoting her Italian ancestry. She wore her hair short and never let anyone see her without makeup..

Gently his fingers traced the soft lines of her back and down the crevice of her warm fullness; she arched her back when he touched "The Spot" which he came back to repeatedly, tantalizingly.

She rolled onto her back in submission. Running his tongue slowly from her breasts down her thighs he felt her shiver with anticipation. The ecstasy became too much for her to control, she avalanched into a sustained shudder and a series of deep breaths.

Taking his muscular shoulders in her hands she pulled him on top of her. "Again," she whispered, "Take me again." His lips found hers and he obeyed. She wasn't asking now, she was demanding. They became one at the duet, flowing together as the sopranos sang "Viens Marliga" their bodies rising and falling with the voices.

Later they were languishing in that marvelous intimacy that follows lovemaking, the afterglow. Nestling down into the covers she sighed against his thick pecs feeling safe, aroused by his scent. She was still surprised at how she responded to this marvelous man. Raised catholic there were so many "no-no" tapes playing in her subconscious. This had all changed after meeting Mike. Now, after listening to him, when she prepared herself for lovemaking she was fastidious in her bathing, powdering and perfuming in all the special places. She even wore her jewelry to bed as he had told her the courtesans of old used to do.

"I didn't realize how wonderful sex could be until I met you," she whispered. "I'm so ambivalent. I'm a Eucharistic Minister you know. Sometimes, sitting with the other officers of the church I feel so guilty. I often wonder what they would think of me for having sex out of marriage." He held her closer saying nothing realizing the sluice gates of her psychological dam had been opened. He waited patiently to see what would flow out.

"My husband was brought up the same way. He once told me that as a boy his most common admission in the confessional was that he had "touched himself in an impure manner. And I, being a dutiful catholic wife with no sex education, took up his morals. But you my paragon of gallantry pushed past my fear and guilts." She snuggled closer into his neckline kissing along the way. "You drive me to dizzying heights."

"I was raised in an Italian-catholic family," she went on. "I was told that sex was something that nice girls didn't think about. I lived a lot with my Italian grandmother who filled me with fears of the hereafter. She meant well but I can hear her raspy voice with its incantations about the evils of sex and the divinity of purity. She never loved my grandfather, it was an arranged marriage and sex to her was hateful. And of course the nuns were of no help. I, like many catholic women, was sent into marriage not prepared to manage in the honeymoon bed."

"Are you all right with the way we are now?" He asked.

"I'm getting there but I feel guilty because I get angry feeling I was lied to as a young woman. And I shouldn't get angry. But now I understand the book a friend gave me to read. It talked about catholic wives being good targets for men wanting affairs. It said the women were eager once they realized they had never experienced really good, really deep sex like I have with you. I didn't know I could have so many orgasms until you made love to me. I realize now I should have been more active and open with my husband. I should have given him sex more often.

That's not to say I didn't enjoy sex, I did. But we got into bed, had a little patting, I waited dutifully for him to climax then we went to sleep. I sometimes can't believe I enjoy oral sex so much when I used to think of it as dirty." She paused, deep in thought. "Being with you has made me realize how wholesome it can be. You have ruined me for all other men," she, whispered into his ear tracing the inside with the tip of her tongue.

As she talked he had been busy with the tip of his index finger. Her body responded involuntarily as she became moist and warm. As he felt her tense he increased the rhythm and when she clamped her legs together he increased the speed with the tip of his finger driving her wild. Rita cried out "Oh Sweet Jesus" as she shuddered and said, "That's enough Mike honey that's enough." Something in the way she said it caused him to continue. "I can't do it again honey", she protested weakly but not moving away. He felt the telltale increased gripping of his arm and once again moved up and down increasing the speed as her breath came more quickly. "Oh, oh God," she repeated as her body shook again. When she collapsed against him he surrounded her with his arms and held her while she rested, kissing his neck repeatedly.

"You really enjoy sex you know and you are a marvelous lover. Have you always been this active with women?" she murmured drowsily, the endorphins taking over. He said nothing as he continued rubbing her back up around the neck. He made his touch lighter as he stroked her back in a circular, loving motion to keep the after-glow going. As he listened to her soft breathing a feeling of discomfort came over him as though there were an impending doom, he shrugged it off.

READING FROM ISAIAH

They were sitting in front of the bedroom fireplace, enrobed in heavy, soft white robes sipping coffee he had just made. She was fascinated as she had watched him grind the coffee beans recently received from Hawaii. The aroma of the fresh beans being processed filled the room and she had kept sniffing the air. "I can't believe how good that smells," she said. "I'm beginning to not feel guilty for enjoying life anymore."

"Catholics and Jews are inculcated with guilt from the beginning of their lives," he mused. "You, for an example, are born in sin. They have you in an ecumenical grip from the time you leave the vagina. Jews are just as bad and walk on eggs never able to feel they have lived up to expectations. When Emperor Constantine invented Katholikos, it evolved into a method and means of controlling the human spirit. The concept of Sin evolved also as a way to guarantee the faithful would always be plentiful. She rose up, rested on one elbow to look into his face. He always reminded her of Clark Gable with its dark handsomeness and bright smile. She asked, "Don't you believe in sin either?"

"Sinn, in ancient Babylon, was the chief god in charge of all other gods or the boss if you prefer," he responded. "To get rid of people worshipping Sinn the priests used misdirection. If you did something evil they said you "sinned" meaning you did what the god Sinn would do and thus did they stamp him out. If you seriously consider the Ten Commandments you soon realize their purpose. Being impossible to keep, they guarantee that "believers" must return for forgiveness. Its effectiveness is exemplified by the pharmaceutical industry that set up its own commandments."

She scrunched up her face and asked, "Now what does that all mean? You always confuse me so."

"Consider the report your doctor goes over with you when you have a blood test. There are various and sundry items such as WBC, RBC and TSH with each showing ranges it should fall within. Suppose for example your Thyroid Suppression Hormone is 6.1 and the chart says it should fall between 0.4 and 4.5. At that moment the doctor spews forth those hallowed words, "Here, take this" as he hands you a prescription for Levothyroxine. Most do not question the origination point of the standards. Who, for example, says it should be between 0.4 and 4.6? Is it in the bible, one of the commandments? It may as well be since most people obligingly head to the local Osco, get the pills so ordered, and began gulping them according to instruction. What they should do is ask "Why?" and go to the Internet if they know how."

Rita listened with her face showing genuine interest as she always did during his verbal diatribes.

"The pharmaceutical industry," he continued, "noting the success of Sin copied the concept and set up standards which like the Ten Commandments, could not all be met. In this manner they have become immensely wealthy, as has the church, with adherents who question not."

Rita sat back in her chair, studied him for a minute, and then said, "You don't believe the Ten Commandments are meant to be kept then?"

"Absolutely not," Mike responded vehemently. "Take for example the admonition 'Thou Shalt Not Bear False Witness. Suppose you are a mother with a son hiding from authorities in your basement. A squad of terrorists busts in demanding to know the whereabouts of your son, the traitor, so they can kill him; this has actually happened many times. Do you tell the truth, point them to the basement, or do you bear false witness and say you don't know?

Once again she looked at him silently turning the information over in her mind.

Mike continues, "And let's consider 'Thou shalt not kill' in this world where the only way to not be invaded is to kill the would-be invaders; the only way to enjoy a hamburger is to kill a cow. How practical is that?"

"Sure but Father says each one has an explanation," she countered with a lack of enthusiasm. It always irritated Mike to hear someone call another man Father when there was no blood relationship whatsoever and he answered her in an obviously irritated tone.

"Now you are going to the "Ya Buts."

"What's a Ya But," she asked defensively leaning forward again, her face very close to his. He reacted involuntarily to her woman scent and her breasts showing through the open robe but suppressed any action for the moment.

"Ya Buts' are used by those who assume religious authority over others to convince them they, and only they, really have the answers, the combination it takes to get into heaven. When you point out that it says we shouldn't kill and ask about animals for slaughter they haul out the 'Ya But' here's what it really means. Many don't really believe all they preach but the authority, the comfort, sometimes the wealth and power they derive from their 'Let's Pretend' game is too good to give up.

The dumbest kid on the block can all get immense power by simply becoming a minister, rabbi or priest."

She pulled away from him now. "I don't like it when you talk about my religion like that she pouted. You do it too often. You know how I enjoy my church and you promised not to discuss it with me again."

Mike relented, remembering her need for her faith. "I'm sorry and you are right, I did say I wouldn't discuss it with you." He changed the subject to her family and they quietly enumerated the various successes obtained by her children. "Dam," he said, "I just remembered the phone rang while we were upstairs and I haven't checked the message yet. I'll be right back. The fickle finger of fate was about to interrupt their idyllic interlude.

IT BEGINS

Mike went into his den, sat at the desk and punched the "Play" button. The message was from the Cary police department leaving a number which he dialed. A voice came on the line and Mike told him he was returning a call. "Mr. Granite?" The voice inquired.

"What can I do for you?" he responded with his usual caution

"This is Sergeant Mc Evoy of the Cary police department in Cary, Illinois. Are you related to a Leslie Martin? We found your name and phone number in her purse. "

Mike stood upright, his motion knocking over the cup, spilling coffee over his desk blotter. He grabbed a few Kleenex tissues from a box as he attempted to sop up the mess and talk at the same time.

"I am an acquaintance," he answered, "her father was a personal friend of mine. What's the problem? Why do you have her purse?" he asked as he sat back down his face showing anxiety. Rita had followed him into the room and ignoring the fact that her robe had come open made a face and air mouthed, "What's wrong honey?" but he waved her to silence.

"I'm afraid I have bad news for you," came the response he had heard so often on TV crime shows. "Mrs. Martin is in the hospital and her children are dead," this last given in a subdued tone.

Mike had resolved not to respond in a typical fashion and asked quietly, "How did it happen? What are the circumstances?"

"Well sir, we aren't positive but we think the perpetrators may have been part of a group known as the Irish Travelers or White Gypsies," he began. "They travel through an area fleecing the unsuspecting public through bogus roof and driveway repairs. They are notorious for cheating the public and in particular the elderly.

"Where do they come from?" asked Mike.

"As far as I know they started in Ireland. When Cromwell devastated Ireland in 1600 many of the farmers became Gypsies to exist and immigrated to the States during the Potato Famine. They even have their own language called Shelta and Cant. Their living quarters, many sumptuous, are in Augusta, North Carolina. Their children are actually raised to be deceitful, however, not usually violent.

"What leads you to think it was them? Mike inquired. Rita noiselessly air-mouthed another question and again he waved her to silence putting up one finger to indicate he needed time.

"There was a group reported in the area around the time of the murder," replied the officer. "By the way," he continued, "The lady is in Centegra Hospital just outside of Woodstock."

Mike informed the sergeant that he had been a friend to a Marines Corps officer, now deceased, and had promised to look in on his family from time to time. The victims were his daughter and grandchildren. That explained his name being in her book of persons to contact. He told him he would get to the hospital right away and check in with the lady's immediate family.

Giving Rita a quick rundown while he dressed Mike told her he would call her later with all the details. She dressed separately and left after kissing him goodbye. It took Mike less than an hour to get to the hospital. He had heard it was an impressive building and so it was. The outside was a light brown stone with a front entrance sheltered by a canopy for offloading patients in inclement weather. Parking in the visitor's lot he inquired at the front desk and was escorted to the surgery waiting room by a polite guest services representative who told him that Leslie was in surgery. There was an attendant present who asked if he wanted coffee, offered directions to the cafeteria and pointed out an accumulation of magazines on one of the tables distributed throughout the comfortably appointed room. She was truly concerned about the well being of the hospital's visitors and obviously well trained to see to their needs. Mike declined sitting back to observe the others in the room. A man and a woman he called "mother" sat in front of him and talked unceasingly about health foods, Jesus Christ and the healing power of prayer.

A lady who had been sitting with a young woman and an older man got up, went to a paisley couch, and stretched out to sleep. A gentleman who obviously sat at too many dinner tables struggled to get out of his chair. He lumbered upward like an elephant rises reaching for his cane to steady himself. Once up he tested each leg then his back to see if they were going to hold him. They held and he told the attendant he was going to the cafeteria. 'Of course you are.' Mike thought to himself. She gave him a pager to carry advising him it would light up and vibrate if she paged him.

Later the man and his mother stood just outside the door talking with a doctor whose words reduced the woman to tears. Mike heard the attendant discretely suggest they might want the privacy of the chapel located on the lower floor; they left apparently taking the advice. He was uncomfortable in hospitals, his anxieties bringing up unwanted feelings.

Periodically the attendant would direct someone into the waiting room to talk to a doctor and other times simply give out messages she received from the recovery area.

Mike closed his eyes, which turned on the projector of his mind playing over and over the tragedy as it was described to him. "Mr. Granite?" the soft voice startled him. He focused on the lady physician complete in scrubs who leaned towards him. He nodded assent. "Mr. Granite I understand Leslie's parents haven't arrived so I'm sorry to have to tell you that Leslie has passed away. I am so sorry for your loss," then she left. The lines in his face deepened as he took in the information. Misery dug a deep channel in his soul into which all other feelings drained leaving him an empty shell of despair. Leslie's parents hadn't arrived from California so he felt he could make decisions, which they could override if they found them not to their satisfaction.

"Where do I go to make funeral arrangements?' he inquired of the attendant. She directed him to the business office on the second floor where they explained that the body would be taken to the Morgue awaiting pickup by the funeral parlor. He told the clerk that her parents would make all financial arrangements and that he was here to see only to undertaker selection. There were two in town from which he selected the one recommended by the business office. As he walked down the hall to the main entrance he saw two security guards pushing a gurney. This one was completely enclosed with a cover of green plastic. He wondered if it were Leslie being taken down to the morgue.

An hour later he sat in the office of the Lawson Funeral Home listening to the manager, a dour man dressed in morning clothes and further cloaked in a superficial air of concern, drone on and on about how he would have to do nothing, placing a virtual arm around his shoulder, a gesture that invited him to sob. Mike interrupted this canned delivery with "Pardon me sir but you will not take over. I am not disabled with grief and am quite capable of handling the situation and will do so at my own speed, now let's talk cost."

"Oh Mr. Granite," than man blurted his pencil mustache bobbing when he talked, "I didn't mean to upset you…

"Fine," Mike interrupted, "Now let's get on with it. There will likely be a closed casket service in her church so we will not need a viewing room. And the announcements and other brochures you have in this package will not be necessary. I am interested only in embalming and transportation costs." He found himself irritated over the unceasing melodramatic background music designed to tear your heart out.

"Well Mr. Granite," the words oiled out of his mouth preparing a slippery way for Mike to descend and open his wallet, "There is no way we can reduce the charges as everything is planned in the package, we have no provision for breaking things out. You see sir everybody needs announcements, notification and mementos of the occasion. Everyone wants to remember this sad, sad happening and they do so with your graciousness of giving the items that will become so dear to their hearts."

Mike studied the man's face looking for some sign of the smirk he knew had to be there; this wallet-opening attempt under the guise of caring just how he felt was irritating as hell.

"You can talk to the parents," he snapped, "Now let's talk about a casket.

Somewhat ruffled with the chastisement however mild the man kept his composure commensurate with the professional that he was. "If you will follow me sir we can go below to see the display." Rising he caressed the air just behind Mike's left shoulder in a phantom air-push towards the door. Once in the hall he took the lead and headed down a stairway. Mike followed him down and through double doors into a well lit and appointed viewing room.

There were caskets of every size, shape and material in a room about the size of a basketball court. He was shown caskets ranging in price from $15,000.00 to $8,000.00 with clinical psychology applied in such pitches as "We know you will want the dear departed to be well protected as she sleeps" and other such drivel designed to shrink your bank account.

Mike noticed an area they hadn't approached against a bare brick wall in the rear of the room. There, melodramatically illuminated by a yellowing bulb, sat what looked like a basic, wooden casket with little trim. Mike sauntered over to it, looked down into the interior of silk sheeting. Hearing the salesman come up behind him he asked, "And this one, how much is it?"

"Oh sir," he almost wailed, "Oh you wouldn't want that. That is for the indigent we are often asked to take care of *pro bono!*" He's good, thought Mike waiting for the next derisive gem which came immediately. "Something like that can leak and the last thing a person wants is a loved one lying in water for eternity."

Mike studied the man again. He had mouthed this last preposterous platitude with gagging sincerity and Mike wondered how he could keep from laughing.

"Sir," mocked Mike, "When you're dead you don't give a dam what you are laying in. Besides I may find out she wanted to be cremated from her family. What would it take to rent a casket?"

The man's face crumbled into dismay, "Oh sir, we can't rent out a casket."

"Why not?" Mike inquired,

This purveyor of pacification thought for a minute and out came, "Well what if someone had a communicable disease? You wouldn't want your loved one in such surroundings now would you?"

Mike stared in disbelief at what this numb-nuts was saying then decided it was time to end this nonsense. He told him what hospital held the remains and assured him the bill would be paid but to add nothing not agreed to and left. He felt the need for coffee and, having heard about the Woodstock Square went into town and finding a Starbucks, ordered a plain "Hi Octane" as he called like to call it. Seating himself by a far corner he pondered how such a loss affects people. His mind went to his own losses.

Taylor, Michigan 1941

The briquette stove, the only heat in the house, radiated warmth into the room as Mike sat listening to the radio on the 24th of November 1941. It was the only other room besides the tiny bedroom and kitchen with much of the small area being taken up by the stove. Mike slept upstairs in the attic, which had just enough boards down to hold his bed. There was no insulation and in the wintertime he often found little pyramids of snow on the floor when he jumped from the warm covers to rush down to the stove.

It was quite a change from living in Stanley Court, a block or two north of Grand River Avenue in Detroit, Michigan. There they had a nice apartment, one of several in a "U" Shaped complex. The front room had led into a dining room and then into the kitchen; there were three bedrooms upstairs. It never seemed crowded, except on occasions like the evening his mother had someone come in with pots and pans who made dinner for many of the people living in the court area hoping to sell some of the cookware. And it was conveniently located in the city. He and his best buddy, Freddie Kelly could roller skate to the Olympia Stadium, the name of which was changed to "Joe Lewis Stadium", when the "Brown Bomber" became popular. They would hang out there whenever they weren't playing marbles or shooting imaginary bad guys with rubber guns. One would be Hoppalong Cassidy and the other Hoot Gibson the two famous cowboys of the times.

Freddie was Irish Catholic, which in that neighborhood put him a number of steps above Mike who was raised with no particular religion. Taller than Mike with his blonde hair and vee shaped smile it made him appear more Scandinavian than Gaelic. Mike had often heard him use the term sin and hell but never paid much attention, as they were unimportant, more to the point, had no place of concern in his young life. Freddie's mother was a quiet lady separated from her husband and his demon rum, who seemed often to worry about everyone's soul being in a state of grace. Freddie's father used to say that God invented whiskey so the Irish wouldn't take over the world.

Freddie had an Aunt he loved dearly, one who never forgot his birthday, always brought him a Holloway candy bar or little wax bottles filled with sweet liquid, which he shared with Mike, when she came to visit. She was the one who showed him how to make a scooter out of an old orange crate, a two by four and one roller skate. Apparently this lovely lady was a homosexual and due to societal pressures had made a personal decision to take her own life. They were sitting on a curb next to an ice wagon when Freddie looked at Mike and sobbed, "My mom said her soul is going to hell and she can't be buried in any Catholic cemetery. And when they do bury her they will put up a black cross." The tears were pouring out now. Mike had spent the day consoling his friend and he missed being with Freddie the most.

Mike's mother had married Pete Trout, a truck driver for Roadway Transit Company who became a border when she was renting out rooms in the large house on Stanley Avenue just off Fourteenth Street before moving to Stanley Court. He was a nice enough guy with a minimal vocabulary and he had a habit of studying himself in the mirror, puffing out his chest while he flexed his arms in admiration of what he saw. He was not very tall, had heavy shoulders and hairy chest; he drank a little too much. Apparently they had a need to own property as they found this tiny shack in Taylor, Michigan on Koths street, purchased it, and they moved in that spring. There was a two-seater outhouse just out back and the pump for water was also outside. He never thought about missing indoor plumbing; he just went about the business of being a boy.

He met and became friends with a boy living a few houses down, Donald Sinclair, a boy who was born in the area and was in his class at school. Donald loaned him a gun and took him hunting for the first time. While moving through a small thicket he pointed up to a nest and directed Mike to shoot into it, which he did. A little squirrel tumbled out landing at Mike's feet and he asked Don what they should do with it. "Nothing," he said, "It's too small." Mike handed him the shot gun and told him he didn't like hunting, turned and went home.

School was Melvindale High, a long bus ride from his home. He met and immediately liked Mary Riddering, daughter of Superintendant of Schools George Riddering. She had a cheerful disposition and took to Mike right away. He would never forget the day Mr. Strong, the Biology teacher, took them on a field trip just outside the school which was located in a very rural setting. While seeking signs of wild life, at the urging of Mr. Strong, Mary suddenly began clamoring. "Mr. Strong, Mr. Strong, what is this?" she yelled excitedly. "I think I've found a bird's nest. They had been studying the nesting habits of various winged creatures and most recently the tubular structures built by some of the Finches that hung down like a stocking.

They all headed in her direction with Mr. Strong leading the way. As Mike got closer he recognized that what the sheltered Miss Riddering had come across was a condom that someone had carelessly thrown out of a car window following an amorous interlude. When Mike got close enough he recognized it, turned, and headed away from the crowd.

Mr. Strong had a devil of a time explaining away this treasure and Mike had his friends had spent the balance of the morning laughing about the "Riddering Baloon."

Mike's romantic life had been enriched by Louise Ferrante who lived across the gravel road. They were into hugging and kissing but she persistently resisted his attempts to go further. She had the warm nature of Italians and the large, firm breasts of a woman. At gatherings with other school kids they would play "Spin the Bottle" and "Post Office" concentrating on each other. Often on a summer night they would sit on a blanket in his front yard "making out." When they kissed he would fondle her which she allowed just long enough before pushing his hands away. His world was good but heading for a drastic change.

November came blowing in with an icy chill that made the grass crunch when he walked on it. The house was warm as long as the stove was kept full of briquettes. Mike approached his mother with a look of consternation on his face. He wanted advice but it was a delicate subject.

She was busy in the kitchen getting a turkey ready for tomorrows Thanksgiving meal so was a captive audience. "Mom," he started, "Mom, I haven't gone to the bathroom, you know, number two, for three days now." Embarrassed, he waited and then continued when there was no immediate response. "If I don't get rid of something I won't be able to eat tomorrow like I always do, you know, a lot." He looked at her expectantly.

Clarice Curtis Trout was forty-four years of age, short, a little overweight and the type of woman who took care of her children. To this end she rented larger houses taking in borders to supplement her income as a waitress and piano player in bars. Michael used to watch her dye her hair black so as to hide the grey. She was in her third marriage and has always worked hard seeing to it her boys always had food, clothing and a warm home.

An accomplished pianist she used this talent along with waitressing to stay off welfare. In a print dress with an apron she was right off a cover of Good Housekeeping magazine. "Well," she said smiling at him," I understand your concern about the eating. You and Pete always stuff yourselves and you wouldn't be able to do that, now would you?"

"No," he responded slowly, hoping for the cure-all solution. She looked at him for a minute with understanding then went on."I will fix my hot water bottle and you can take it out to the outhouse and it should take care of your problem." He stared at her. He had often seen the red, rubber container wondering why it was called a bottle when it was flat. It had a hose coming out of the bottom that ended in a black, hard rubber tube of some sorts. He had heard of enemas but cringed at the idea. He watched as she prepared the device thinking of the wind howling outside and the way it would come through the cracks of the outhouse, he shivered. "Now you take this end and shove it into your rectum and...

"Oh Mom," he protested, "Don't go into detail." She understood his embarrassment and continued. "Once you have it in, you release this clamp here and the water solution will go into you. Let it go in, all of it, before you removed the end, then sit down and everything should be all right. Oh yes, you have to hold the bottle up over your head to get it flowing just right."

Totally embarrassed by now Mike put on his coat and hat then took the bottle from her and headed out the door not entirely sure of what he was about to do. Leaves were skittering across the frozen ground as the wind blew them, and him, on a zig zag course. Reaching the door of the outhouse with the little crescent moon carved in the top he turned the piece of wood that held it shut. The door opened revealing the plank with the two holes and even in this weather smelled like a toilet. Mike entered and then put the end of the hook through the nail that had been bent over to keep the door shut; it was cold, very cold out there. The little building made of discarded lumber moved in the wind gusts.

Getting his pants down was no problem, getting the dam thing in was another matter. First he sat and tried to insert it with his right hand, trying to hold the bottle high with his left hand. That didn't work because he couldn't get his hand with the end far enough back when he tried to place it between his legs. "Dam it" he protested. Trying every which way he finally decided he would have to bend over, insert the end, then scoot up onto the cold wooden seat hoping all the while he didn't get a sliver in his ass. "Shit" he muttered not realizing he had made somewhat of a joke, as that was what he was after.

Bending over opened his underside to the frigid air and he goosed himself silly trying to find the opening and hold the bottle up at the same time. Finally, finally he got it in, hunched his buttocks up so that he was in position and with more than just a little fear released the spring catch. Immediately the warm solution filled his bowel and he let out a yelp when he thought his belly was going to burst. He pulled out the end just in time as his bowel released its matter and with it, his concern; there would be lots of turkey tomorrow.

He sat there a moment feeling fluid drip out and begin to freeze. A smile appeared across his face, and why not, he had conquered his problem, he was free to eat all he wanted tomorrow, and to a young boy, that is a most important thing. Life was good. He would fill his belly then lie on the rug in front of the radio and listen to The Lone Ranger followed by The Green Hornet.

On December 7, 1941 President Franklin Delano Roosevelt proclaimed "An Unlimited State of National Emergency" during his "Day of Infamy" speech. Japan had attacked America by bombing Pearl Harbor even as their envoy was in Washington talking peace. They had joined with Germany and Italy to form the "Axis" and were expanding the Japanese

Empire at a rapid rate. In August of 1942 it would extend northeast to the Aleutian Islands of Alaska, West to Burma and South to what is now Indonesia. The Imperial Japanese army appeared to be unbeatable. They had killed thousands, occupied China and captured key islands around the Pacific. At the same time the seemingly unstoppable German Army was conquering all of Europe while Italy went after Africa and territory easily reached from Italian soil. This tragedy would pale when compared to what was going to happen to Mike.

Mike's brother Lee, six years older, had remained in Detroit, living with a friend and would wind up somewhere in Italy with the Army Blue Devil Division. His best friend, Freddie Kelly would be killed in The Black Forest campaign in Germany in 1944. America had lost its navy and everyone was suddenly afraid.

The small kitchen, in the small house on the small plot of land in Taylor, Michigan was warm with the love of the Christmas holiday. There was the fresh aroma of cream-of-wheat with brown sugar permeating the air. The warm cinnamon toast was slathered with butter and cups of hot chocolate made this into a virtual gingerbread house.

Young Michael felt good as he looked out the window past the two-hole outhouse and into the back woods. Deer often came down from there and he particularly wanted to see them today. Not that he believed in Santa Claus since he had found the red sled hidden in the coal bin when they lived on Hooker Avenue in Detroit. The following year his first stepfather whom he loved left their family before Christmas, driving off with Mike crying and begging him to stay. It was a huge loss for an eight-year-old boy who called him Dad and considered him his father. After losing two fathers, the first when he was but two years old, his mother was more important than ever. She was all he had. They ate and laughed and talked about the trip into Detroit this afternoon to see old friends.

He and his mother bundled up and walked arm in arm the distance of about half a mile before leaving for Detroit where they were going to spend Christmas Eve with friends. They talked quietly as they walked past rows of dry corn stalks whispering to each other in the breeze. Reaching the top of Martins Hill she wrapped him in her coat her cheek next to his ear, her softness and smell assuring his young soul that this would be a good Christmas. They stood together quietly a woman and son looking at Halloran's pond. The ground sloped to the water's edge ending in a moving mosaic of geese and ducks commenting loudly on their upcoming trip south.

She nuzzled his ear making him laugh and whispered the gentle nonentities that mothers have uttered for years to soothe and show love. As they stood snow wafted out of the slate-gray sky enrobing the landscape in a white negligee. A deer with her fawn walked casually in front of them, stopped to look at their immobile figures, then pranced off down to the pond.

"Mom," spoke Michael, "Sometimes you don't always seem happy."

Turning him gently by the shoulders so he faced her she kissed his forehead, looked into his eyes and replied, "Your grandmother died on Christmas Day years ago in Maywood, Illinois and I sometimes remember the experience that's all. Not to worry though because it soon passes." They returned to the house and got ready to leave heading into a day that would give the young lad more anguish than anyone deserved, anguish that would leave him broken-hearted, lost and enmeshed in a sexual intrigue that would rival anything put out by Hollywood.

A burst of laughter brought him back to the present. He paid his bill and continued the journey home.

MINDY

Mike awoke early and lay quietly as he contemplated the funeral he had to attend in two days. He thought of Rita, who had called to say she was going to Florida to visit her ninety eight year old mother, then got up and put on his robe. In the kitchen he opened the sealed container that held coffee beans, put two tablespoons in the grinder and pulsed it until they were reduced to large chunks; he inhaled the fresh ground aroma with a smile. Later, sipping coffee on the back deck, he listened to the geese talking, the crows yelling instructions and the cacophony of frogs croaking from the pond just to the south of the house. Through the comforting sound of nature he also heard the chugging of Warren Martin's tractor out on the front ten acres. Mike had bought twenty acres a few years ago and he let his neighbor Warren grow hay for his dairy herd at no charge. He got up, dressed and went down the walk towards the field.

Warren sat astride his old Harvester tractor with the peeling red paint and the manure scoop on the front. Like his vehicle he was squat and powerful with fingers the size of small sausages. Always amiable and quick to laugh he was the kind of man that could fix the world if you gave him a piece of baling wire. His wife Joan sold eggs around town and his two boys helped with the chores. Mike ambled over to chat and Warren turned the tractor off when he saw him coming. "Hey there good friend what's new?" Mike asked.

"Well now I'll tell ya ," Warren replied, "Joanie and I saw Mindy Mason the other day, "She says that her husband Bob has himself a little honey away from home and they are separated. She is really upset." He was referring to Bob Mason who owned a number of businesses around the county and his pretty wife Mindy.

Mike responded with the usual amenities about the tragedy of marital break-ups then they chatted about the weather and crops before he headed back to the house; he had purposely cut the visit short when he heard about Mindy. She was a pretty blonde woman, not very tall, perhaps five feet four with a perky way of saying "Hieee" in a tone that slid up an octave. She had a great personality sitting on top of the largest melon-like breasts he had ever seen. They were so firm looking he was sure you could sit flowerpots on them and they would hold.

He recalled how his ex-wife Mary regretted having small breasts and Mike had made her feel good by stating that anything over a mouthful was wasted. One day in their kitchen Mary asked Mindy if those were really all her. Mindy responded by pulling up her shirt revealing a bra straining to hold two extremely large mounds of very firm flesh. *Dam, I wonder what it would be like to bury my face it that he thought.* He suspected it would be possible, as Mindy was quite a tease. Once, upon hearing he had bought Mary a color TV, she began kidding him about what she would have to do so she could get a TV. Something about the way she said it caused him to feel she was more than just kidding. Also whenever she came over she would come out into the yard give him a lingering hug and talk with him alone. Mindy hugged every man she met; it was her way of claiming a little bit of another woman's man.

After he and Mary had been divorced five years Mindy called him one evening. "Hi," she said all bubbly, "I thought I would just say hello and see what you were up to these days." Her approach caused Mike to think she wanted to get together, perhaps have an affair but lacked the courage to come right out with it. He suspected she had been drinking due to her speech. Then she dropped the hook into the water. "I've always wanted to ask," she said, "Are you as good in bed as Mary tells me you are?" His imagination soared and he went for the bait.

"Why don't we get together here at my place and you can find out?" he had asked. "Or I can come over to your house any time."

Oh no," she had declined, "I couldn't do that to Bob. It would bother me too much. I couldn't keep it secret." Try has he would Mike couldn't get her to agree to a tryst of any type and so he had ended the conversation. He attributed it to her loneliness and phone sex was safe after all. Apparently it took all the courage she had just to make the call. Following through was too much to expect. A few days later he met her in the local store and was surprised to see she had lost a lot of weight.

This information from Warren about her marital breakup renewed his interest. He came up with a plan to call and pretend it was for the simple purpose of wishing them good holidays. He figured she would mention the breakup and he could then move into the subsequent seduction. When he called their machine came on. "HI you guys," he spoke into the phone, "I came across your names in my book and thought it time I wished you a happy holiday." She phoned him that same evening. Bringing up the subject of her separation she sobbed a little as she told him of her husband deciding he wanted his younger secretary. They arranged to meet the following Monday evening at Armando's restaurant just across from the local theatre in town. It was a relatively new place having many tables flanked by a wall of booths; all tables had checkered table cloths and all prices were high.

He stood waiting outside enjoying the cool air while he read the marquee on the theatre across the street next to the picture framing business. He spotted her walking toward him and could see that she had gained much of her weight back and was without makeup.

She wore a grey sweat suit and had no coat, obviously not made up to impress anyone. She hugged him and as usual her breasts were inviting. Once they were seated she began to cry softly explaining her feeling of rejection and the attendant depression. In between tears she explained that Bob had told her he was having an affair with this lady who worked for him and wanted a divorce. He was claiming to be penniless but she felt he had upwards of five million dollars since he owned several Laundromats. She kept saying she didn't know what she had done wrong.

"Mindy dear," Mike said, "It isn't a matter of you doing anything right or wrong. You are simply a victim of normal circumstances and Bob has declared war on your marriage. You have got to get ready to inflict casualties."

She looked at him with a sadness born of years of neglect and sobbed quietly. "Oh I can't do anything like that. I don't even have a good car anymore. My old Cadillac needs fixing and Bob won't let me have the eight hundred dollars it's going to cost."

"Well hell, you've got to have a car. I'll lend you the money and you can pay me back out of your settlement…how's that?"

"Oh I couldn't do that," she responded, "I don't know what I'm going to do. That's why I wanted to talk to you." When they had finished their meal he invited her to his place which she declined due to a previous commitment to watch the Bears play at Detroit with a friend. They agreed that she would come to his house the next evening at 7 PM and he would fix dinner. They hugged and kissed good-bye. He wondered if she would be ready to find out just how good he was in bed. Her anger at her soon-to-be Ex made her a prime candidate.

What wasn't obvious at the time was a more sinister problem dogging her every minute of her life; she was addicted to painkillers. Mindy had a very bad back as the result of a traffic accident. Her vehicle was rammed by a garbage truck, the driver of which had been drinking. Mindy suffered whiplash and subsequent pain in her lower back, between the fourth and fifth lumbar.

Surgery was prescribed when a session or two with a good chiropractor might have been all that was needed. The procedure was not successful resulting in many surgeries throughout the years and even a visit to Canada. She was currently in the hands of a group that made multiple injections of a water based fluid into her hip causing her intense pain and excessive use of pain killing medication. Mike didn't know it but Mindy was a prescription drug junkie.

The following evening he prepared the house with candlelight and fixed a fire. After waiting an hour he resigned himself to the fact she wasn't coming and wouldn't call. He was angry and considered her what is euphemistically known as a "Cock Teaser" and that it would be best to leave her alone. In spite of himself he did call the next day however and she explained that had been in court had received such ill treatment by her husband that she cried for hours and stayed with a friend for solace. They agreed to talk again.

It was a few days later that Mindy called. "Mike," she said softly, "During dinner last week you offered to lend me money to have my car fixed. Does that offer still hold?"

"You bet it does Min," he responded, "Everyone needs a car." They agreed she would pick it up a check the following morning.

She arrived about 10 O'clock the next morning dressed in blue jeans and a pullover top looking quite perky; Mindy was a very pretty woman. She had a habit of cocking her head to the side and winking at you that was cute. They hugged and when they kissed she held him so it lasted a long time and was quite passionate. She moved her breasts against him in a way that would awaken a dead man. He showed her what he had done to the house then took her upstairs to show her the fireplace in the master bedroom. He moved behind her shoving his hands up under her top to fondle her breasts. The size and firmness excited the hell out of him. She did not pull away but said, "I'm not very comfortable with this Mike." The words "not very" told him a lot and he suggested they return to the living room.

"What would you like to drink love?" he asked.

"I'll take Seven Up if you have it." A short time later she sat sipping her drink as he wrote out a check. He saw tears in her eyes and moved next to her so as to hold her. As if on cue she began kissing him with an intensity that took him by surprise; she was hungry for loving. During one very passionate kiss he again reached under her top caressing her breasts. "I don't think I;m ready yet Mike," she protested mildly but made no effort to remove his hands. She rested her head on his chest. Keeping her head firm against him she looked up into his eyes and said, "I do like you a lot," and smiled demurely.

It wasn't long before they were kissing again. Kneeling before her he raised her top, reached around behind her and undid her bra in one swift motion. Her breasts tumbled out like melons from a basket as she lay her head back.. His hands seemed small as he cupped them and began enjoying himself to the fullest. He nibbled gently. She took his head in her hands, pulling him into her, smothering him with her warm softness. "Let's go up to my bedroom," he whispered. Without a word she took over, pulling him to his feet, heading towards the stairway.

Standing at the head of his King sized bed she removed her top. Next she stripped down her sweat pants and stood there entirely naked. In a few moments they were in bed wrapped in a passionate embrace. She seemed starved for kisses. Whenever he pulled away she would pull his head back down. Their tongues intertwined as he gently bit her lips and kissed her eyelids. Taking her fullness in his mouth as he gently pulled her leg up over his hip and began stroking her ever so gently with a tickling motion. Her moans told him she was ready but he waited and her kisses became more intense as her body took over as she approached climax.

Kissing her body as he slid down his face was buried in her thighs. He could feel her trembling, With one motion she reached over and virtually lifted him up so that he was on top of her and he entered her effortlessly. "Oh God." She yelled, "Oh God!" as she avalanched in an ecstasy that lasted for a full minute. "I can't stop," she panted, "I can't stop."

Her soft expanse enrobed his loins as they became one. He adjusted his rhythm until she cried out and grasped his hips to pull him further into her and they were lost in each other. It was two hours before they were satisfied. They lay there awhile resting when she said, "Do you feel you have taken advantage of me?"

"I do not," he answered matter-of-factly.

"I've never had multiple orgasms before. Bob and I never made love we just had sex," and she kissed him longingly then rose abruptly saying, "I have to go," and pulled on her shirt and pants and skipped out of the room singing like a bird. *'My God she is delightful.; Mike thought.*

Mindy called that evening to thank him. Her voice was that of a little girl. She would lapse into that persona when pleased. She said she would like to come over again and they arranged for Tuesday evening for dinner. He prepared an asparagus casserole with wild mushroom sauté and found himself waiting anxiously. She arrived about 7 O'clock again dressed in a sweat suit and looking more beautiful than he had ever seen her. After eating she took a pill, which she said she needed so as to not throw up.

During dinner he cautioned her not to engage in conversation about their love making on the phone, as it was too easy for her husband to put a tape recorder on a line. He further told her if she forgot she would find him engaging in small talk about how he enjoyed "chatting" with her with "chatting" being a code word for enjoying sex." She agreed. They watched the movie "An Affair To Remember." At the conclusion he asked if she would like to sit and talk, play Scrabble or go upstairs and make love. Without hesitation she rose, took his hand and pulled him towards the stairs obviously enjoying being in charge.

He put on a Kenny G disc and they enfolded each other as they kissed, their tongues teasing. Mindy's full body was warm and full of passion. Without a word she surprised him by pushing back the covers, moving down as she kissed his legs then took him.

She brought him to the edge then lay back and he responded with controlled rhythm. Once again he slid down too her thighs to drive her wild and he felt her shudder again and again. Later, cradling her head in his arm, Mike lay quietly while she napped. She needed this after-glow, this affection. When she awoke they kissed and she was gone again; just like that.

It was a little after 6 AM the next morning, the day of the funeral, when the phone rang. "Hello," Mike spoke drowsily into the mouthpiece.

"Brush your teeth, I'm on my way," bubbled Mindy.

Somewhat startled all he could think of to say way "Okay" but she had hung up. He brushed his teeth, used an underarm deodorant spray and splashed on what he had learned was her favorite after-shave lotion. It wasn't much longer before she came through the back door, into the kitchen radiant as a new bride. They kissed then Mike dropped to his knees, pulled up her oversized sweatshirt he buried his face in her warm, softness. She reached down and pulled him to his feet while at the same time sinking to her knees. Pulling down his pajama bottom she took him and it didn't take long. "My turn," he said and gently backed her into the sitting room, pulled down her tights and panties together, eased her to the floor hearing her cry out as all of him went into her. They cascaded together immediately with Mindy clutching his so tightly he had hard time breathing. In a matter of minutes, she was gone again. Mike dressed and left for the internment. Mindy was extraordinary, that was for sure.

THE CAMERA

Leslie's parents had taken over the minute they arrived selecting the internment site, notifying him of all particulars when they had dinner together. The father was tall and slim and his eyes reminded Mike of his daughter. He was spending his retirement years playing golf. Her mother, diminutive like her daughter and a little on the heavy side, had the air of a mature, refined woman who was devastated by it all. It was a difficult meeting, one that Mike was glad to see end.

Mike arrived at Arlington cemetery late having gone by the ramp on I 294 that would have taken him directly into the area. Swearing softly he drove over to the Eisenhower where he looped back onto I 294 then got off at the North Avenue ramp. The cemetery was just ahead and he pulled into the area through the wrought iron gates. He located the burial site by slowly circling until he spotted Leslie's parents. Pulling behind a green Chevy he got out and stood staring at the mound of dirt surrounded by flowers. Approaching slowly his ability to hide his feelings eluded him and a single tear ran down his right cheek. The sight of the smaller caskets put a knot in his stomach. *"Christ,"* he muttered, *"a completely innocent family wiped out."*

Standing on a slight hill just west of the crematorium he stared at the three freshly dug graves of his friend's daughter and her children. The police had told him that the crime scene was terrible. The children had been shot and their mother raped then her throat cut. It appeared that whoever had done it had used a straight razor. As far as they could tell there was little suffering. "Little suffering my ass," Mike had retorted. Their canvassing had turned up nothing more than the "the Irish travelers" the police had told him about. They were trying to locate them for interrogation under the supposition one or more of them were responsible.

Shifting his gaze upward he saw the long rows of grave markers running east to the end of the property. The minister began his eulogy. Mike's mind drifted back fifty years to the western slope on Okinawa overlooking a makeshift burial ground...

Marine Lieutenant Mike Granite, stood on a promontory just south of Nago looking down on Okinawa's western shore at columns of dead bodies that ran down to the edge of the sea. There was a warm breeze bringing in the aroma of the ocean and death. The clay was red here and burial details were putting fallen warriors in body bags waiting for burial.

In February of 1944 the technique of "leapfrogging", bypassing islands with large concentrations of Japanese soldiers had saved thousands of lives. It took the Marines north to the Marshall Islands where they captured Kwajalein and Enewetok. They leapfrogged Truk, bombing it instead to make it unusable as an air base and rendering thousands of Japanese soldiers ineffective. In August they had occupied Guam, Saipan and Tinian working through the end of 1944. They then concentrated on Okinawa, gateway to Japan.

The assault on Okinawa, "Project Iceberg", began on April 1st, 1945. It had been called the *tetsu no ame* or "Typhoon of Steel' by the Japanese. This battle would have one of the highest numbers of casualties of any in the war with the Japanese losing well over 100,000 troops and the allies losing 12,000 with 50,000 casualties. Three Marine divisions and the Tenth Army assaulted the island on Easter Sunday called "Love Day" by the Marines; it happened to be April Fools Day as well.

The Sixth Marine Division Reinforced, Mike's division, seized Yontan Airfield, captured Ishikawa Isthmus, the town of Nago and heavily fortified Motobu Peninsula in just 13 days. After extreme loss of life they captured Sugar Loaf Hill, turned south to capture the capital city of Naha then landed on Oruku Peninsula to take Naha Airfield and Harbor after nine days of fierce fighting. Joining the battle lines to the South they destroyed the enemy entrenched in a series of rocky ridges extending to the southern tip of the island. Mike's group was the Sixth Joint Assault Signal Company.

As he looked one of his men spoke. "How many do you figure there are?"

"About 500 as far as I can see," he replied. "Look over there. They are far behind and no chance of catching up. They need to get them in the ground because in this heat putrefaction sets in fast."

"What are they putting into the bags with the bodies?" the young Marine inquired.

"They put each man's identification in a Sake bottle then put that into the body bag just before the burial detail gets to it. It's gonna get worse because our ships are taking more hits every day and Navy corpses are coming in fast. It didn't have to be this way," he said in disgust.

"How's that sir?" the Marine asked.

Mike looked over at him. He was young, eighteen years of age at most, tall, well built and loaded with ammo, K Bar and M1 rifle. "Well Admiral Yamamoto's declared motto of 'One plane for one ship' was working to our advantage. Coming in singly we were able to put up a wall of Ack-Ack fire and knock most of them out of the sky before they could crash into a ship. Our intelligence boys didn't let this information out, as they did not want Yamamoto changing his methods. As luck would have it some newspaper wag with his head up his ass caused the death of hundreds of men by getting hold of the story and releasing it. Once aware, the Admiral began sending planes in four or more at a time. The results were devastating. Hundreds of Navy personnel were killed and over forty ships sunk."

"I wonder if that reporter is aware of how many good men died because of his scoop."

"He wouldn't care," snapped Mike angrily his face taking on a scowl of contempt, "Its accolades he cares about. He wants to get slapped on the back and told what an ace reporter he is. His editors are no better. They dam near kill as many Americans as the Japanese do getting stories and putting them in print. They like to puff up and say the public has a right to know. Horseshit! The public does not need to know until the war is over." Mike stiffened, turned to his men shouting angrily, "Hoist anchor Marines, we're moving out."

They relieved the 7th regiment and established a base along the western flank of Machinato Airfield. Mike stopped a young private coming over a ridge. "Take those dog tags off and tie one through each shoe lace," he ordered. "And put a sock on that canteen so you can draw it out without it making noise and giving you position away at night. You'll get your throat cut soon enough without helping them. The Japs are constantly reconnoitering in the dark, slipping into foxholes and slitting the throats of anyone they can find." Not waiting for a response he led his 45-man platoon toward the Asa Kawa, a tidal river that ended in the East China Sea. His orders were to cross it and carve out a bridgehead then head on to Naha, the capital.

Leading his men through a heavily wooded area he heard a thud and felt something wet splatter over a portion of the back of his neck; it was the brains of one of his men. Another man fell like a poled ox his mouth gaping, also shot in the head. They dropped to the ground and were scanning the area to see where the sniper had his position. They could see nothing. Mike had an idea; he had noticed the shots were in the back of the heads. "OK men move on out", he yelled, "Take over Sergeant," he said to Mc Elroy. When they had moved past him and around the hill out of sight Mike kneeled down behind a bush and waited. It wasn't long before he saw a Japanese soldier coming out of the ground where he had been secreted by a trap-door spider hole. They dug these and covered them with a frame of twigs and grass. After men walked past the hole the soldier would pop up behind them and pick them off one by one.

The soldier spotted Mike immediately and must have run out of ammo as he just stood there holding what Mike recognized as a Type 38 Arasaka rifle. It was an out of date weapon, bolt action and no doubt stamped with the likeness of a Chrysanthemum, the Emperor's insignia. It was five and a half feet long with the bayonet making it unwieldy for the short man to negotiate. His mouth was open in a sort of grimace showing a number of gold implants in his front teeth. Mike saw a snarl but he also saw fear; this was no Bushido warrior, this was a peasant farmer put into service for pillage and rape.

Mike could have pumped a round into him but instead ordered him to surrender in Japanese. The Jap started towards him. Once again Mike ordered him to surrender knowing that *Seishin* or "fighting spirit" would probably not allow it. The man lunged at him with his bayonet and he parried with his own. The weapons clanged as it bounced to the side. Mike considered putting a round in his chest and ending it but instead he said "All right Tojo let's see what you've got," and went into a fighting stance; left foot out in front, weapon held with left arm only partially extended, ready to thrust forward.

They stood facing each other, circling slowly, each trying to find an advantage. The Nip was about his height, had a scar running from his right ear down to his chin and he held his weapon unsteadily with both hands elevated to Mike's heart position periodically pushing forward, looking for an opening. Mike became icy calm, dropped his gaze so that he was looking at the man's testicles then feigned a lunge at them causing the inexperienced soldier to drop his weapon to parry. That was the last mistake he would ever make.

At this point Mike rotated his bayonet to his left, then up and across slicing across the man's throat with razor sharp tip, severing his jugular and tearing his throat open. Mike stared dispassionately as blood poured over the soldier's uniform. Slowly he dropped to his knees then keeled over his forehead resting on Mike's combat boot. Mike got the toe of his boot under the body, raised it up and pushed forward causing it to fall into an incline and disappear from view. "There ya go Tojo," he said, "Some Gyrene will probably come along and kick out those gold choppers you're sport'n."

Mike looked up as a car horn beeped him back to the present seeing just the opening of the graves, the bodies having been interred. He moved toward the family to pay his respects. The father, dressed in a grey overcoat was wearing a white shirt with black tie and was placing his Homburg back on his head. The Mother, dressed in a heavy black wool coat, was wearing a warm scarf wrapped around her neck. They conversed quietly, exchanged pleasantries, commiserated about the unfairness of life and Mike left. As he strolled towards his car he turned around to take a last look at the site.

Leaves skated across patches of ice as a chill wind caused him to shiver even more. The ceremony was over; he stood alone weeping inwardly at this loss. This young woman and her sweet children butchered by some piece of human shit. His stomach was churning and he knew he had to do something, anything about this rage he was feeling. Turning abruptly he looked into the face of one of the gravediggers standing politely off to the side. The man nodded slightly to acknowledge his anguish then dropped his head, averting his gaze. Mike walked down the concrete path past the markers until he reached his car. As he opened the door he looked over the roof and could see the men working to complete the burial. Sinking into the seat he had to wait as a column of cars streamed past him on the way to another internment. As he waited a security guard sidled up to his car. He lowered the window.

"Not the best place to be, is it sir?" he offered.

"It surely isn't", Mike answered looking away so as not to prolong the conversation.

"We get up to ten burials a day at times," he stated matter-of-factly.

"That so," said Mike. Sensing the man wanted to talk he pointed to a television cameras overlooking part of the grounds. "Why do they have those? Afraid someone will get away?" he quipped trying a little dry humor.

"Actually they are there to prevent the theft of markers and shrubbery. We had one party that wanted to put plants in a toilet bowl. They figured no one would take it. I heard of one cemetery that lost $30,000.00 worth of Chinese palms. They began spraying them with a concoction from Cornell University called "ugly stuff" which turned the plants a garish pink during the holiday season." Mike's gaze froze on the image of the camera "god-dam it!' he yelled pounding the steering wheel. "God-dam it how could I forget!" The procession ended. He raced down the narrow road and out onto the street. He was visualizing the video camera security system he had installed for Leslie, remembering their conversation what seemed a long time ago.

Positive ID

"That is a really a complicated looking device," said Leslie as he held it up for her to see. A lovely blonde lady with smooth tanned skin, she reminded him of a makeup model. She was wearing a yellow blouse over white shorts which showed her lovely, slim legs beautifully.

"It's a high-resolution miniature CMOS television camera built into this motion detector device. It has a built-in transmitter and will be powered by new, internal batteries for up to one year. It has Auto Iris for light variation and even has BLC which is Balance Light Control to compensate for bright spots."

"And of course I know exactly what you are talking about," she kidded.

"I'm going to set it up so that if anyone comes up on the porch it will automatically go into the "Record" mode and it has a transmitter that will turn your VCR on to Record," he explained. "I am placing a little receiver on the back of your VCR that will receive the signal. You must remember to check it each time you come home."

"I'll remember and I can't thank you enough. But you really shouldn't have gone to all this trouble. I don't have any enemies that I know of."

"It isn't enemies I'm concerned with," responded Mike, "It's the unusual, and the unexpected we have to look out for. With this you will know if anyone has come into the house while you are gone. You will also be alerted when you are home." Well she hadn't been alerted and Mike wanted to know why.

He was out of the car the moment it stopped and up the stairs with the spare key she had given him in his hand; the "Crime Scene" tape had been removed long ago. He opened the door and entered. The silence was eerie and brought waves of anger washing over him as he went into the front room. It was clean and neat giving no indication there had ever been atrocities performed here. The "Crime and Trauma Scene Decontamination" or CTS Decon crew had done their job well. . He switched on the VCR that was resting on the television set which had apparently been ignored by the police, rewound the tape then pushed the "Play" button and sat on the couch to see what he had.

As the machine began to play he saw the faces of three men who had obviously come up onto the porch and rang the bell. Mike studied them. One looked to be about forty years old, Latino and slim with a full mustache and black hair that was combed straight back. He was wearing a shirt with the logo 720 Club on the pocket. Next to him was a second man, clean shaven with pock marks and a tooth missing in the front of his mouth.

He had a triangular shaped face with hair that swept up and around a high forehead. A third man stood behind them. He was tall and rawboned with a "Redneck" look about him, sporting a ponytail. Mike took the tape home with him.

Later, watching the tape at home Mike could see the men were talking to someone, perhaps one of the children, they suddenly disappeared, apparently having pushed their way in. He nursed a beer as he watched the tape again and again burning those faces into his memory.

The portable phone next to his chair demanded his attention but he ignored it for a short time, and then picked it up. His Marine buddy Jack Toneg was on the line and said he wanted to come over for a visit. Mike told him to come ahead and continued to watch the video. When Jack he arrived Mike told him of his discovery; Jack was the only one he ever confided in. Actually he called him "Cap'n Jack" as that was his rank when he mustered out. He referred to himself as a Cajun from Louisiana. He served in Korea where he was captured and put in confinement for over ten months. He escaped when the jail he was in was hit by bombs during an air raid. That little stint gave him some bad lungs from the putrid air heavy with mold he was forced to breathe all that time. His ability to speak French however brought him into the limelight during the Viet Nam war so he was put back into active duty. His face got your attention by a prominent DeGaulle type nose over a handle-bar mustache and he reminded Mike of a comedian named Jerry Colona. They sat in Mike's front room in front of the fire. It was a man's room with brown and beige furniture, a short tufted rug on the floor immediately in front of the couch and Mike's medals and awards displayed in a glass framed display case sitting on a shelf attached to the stone chimney. His ceremonial sword hung below them.

"Jack my friend I'm going to tell you something but before I do I want to emphasize how secret it has to be kept. In Intelligence we had a saying that three men could keep a secret if two of them are dead. I need you to tell no one, not your wife, your boy, your minister, no one." Jack assured him he would keep whatever the information was, between the two of them. Mike told him the story.

"Don't you think you ought to turn this information over to the police?" Jack urged.

Mike bristled. "No god-dam it I won't turn these tapes over to the authorities," he responded angrily. "If they catch them they have to convict them providing they don't get off on some technicality. And if they do convict them the "Bleeding Hearts" will insist on no death penalty and in time they might get paroled. They won't kill them because of the "innocent man" syndrome. They wet their pants over the thought they might kill someone for a crime they didn't commit and do you know what burns my ass about that? Mike was standing over Jack like an inquisitor.

"No I don't," said Jack, "But I can see you sure as hell are going to tell me."

Mike walked over to one of the large windows and looked East towards town. "Every year," he began "the "Vaccine Adverse Event Reporting System" gets 11,000 reports. About 1 percent of these are about the deaths of babies as a direct result of getting the DPT shot which is mandated by law, mandated by law!" Mike was yelling now, "And it kills 110 infants each and every goddamn year but you don't see people marching for the DPT shot to be outlawed.

Hell no! They say it is for the good of the many to suffer the loss of an innocent few. So why isn't it acceptable to kill one or two innocent men on death row for the good of the many?"

"I didn't know that," Jack responded pulling at the ends of his mustache. He had settled down in the sculptured leather chair so that his stomach bulged over his belt. He was laboring to breathe today and kept his hand on the oxygen bottle next to him on the floor.

"There is a man right here in town got the shot when he was 14 years old, immediately passed out and to this day has a weak right side, walks with a limp and his muscles have a tendency to get rigid," he continued. "There are thousands like him. And as I said 110 innocent babies die every year", he was pacing now, "because it is for the good of the many but they will let mass murderers go because they might, and that's "<u>might</u>" kill an innocent person. Well how innocent are those babies?"

"I never thought of it that way but it makes sense," Jack responded knowing full well that the best way to handle his friend at a time like this was to remain silent and listen. "You and I have seen hundreds of innocent young men get killed defending their country and that seems acceptable. Innocence has nothing to do with it. I grant you we might execute an innocent man but as you say it is for the good of the many because most of the people on death row are guilty as charged."

Mike settled down into his chair his face dark as a grave. "You're dam right. There aint no recidivism with the death penalty. He picked up his Marine K-Bar combat knife which he kept on the table next to his reading chair and tossed it in the air repeatedly. "If our society would climb out of the dark ages they would handle murderers differently." He was speaking at Jack not to him.

"How's that?" Jack asked.

"When there is incontrovertible proof that a man is a murderer, such as Jeffrey Dahmer or a John Wayne Gacey they should be used to give life to people who need organs. They should be anesthetized and taken into an operating theater. People needing an organ transplant could be lined up in a circle and the operating staffs could then harvest the organs of the murderer. Once done the carcasses would be buried, eight people would have their lives back, and the world would be none the worse, indeed it would be better because of the eight survivors. But we, because of the handwringers, parole them back into society where they kill all over again" He sat down letting his head droop down

What will you do when you find them?" queried jack.

"I don't want to be on record about that," Mike responded darkly.

"Well", said Jack, "It's 7:20 and time to go." Something about what he said made Mike stare at him for a moment, trying to bring something up to the front of his mind; it wouldn't come.

That evening, after Jack left, he reviewed the video many times trying to find clues as to who these men might be and thereby where they might be found. He went to bed. At midnight he sat upright. The words "720 club" had rolled like marbles in front of his sub-conscious eye. The one killer had that on his shirt on the left-hand side above the pocket. He rose, went downstairs and took out the Chicago white-pages phone book. He found it, the 720 club on Wells Street. He would find them one by one. If they had known their fate they would have taken their own lives and been the better for it.

The next evening he was on Rush Street and found the 720 club. Sidling up to the bar he ignored the eyeing he got from a floozy sitting nearby, ordered a Martini and began to chat with the bartender, an affable Irishman with a good sense of humor. They exchanged pleasantries and when the time seemed right Mike described the man he was seeking. He got nothing in the way of information, as the barkeep didn't recall anyone matching Mike's description. Downing his drink he wrote down his phone number for the barkeep and left. Many eyes were upon him as he left one pair in particular.

As soon as he arrived home he watched the video again and bitter vetch collected in his throat as he thought of the massacre. "Shit," he said out loud, "Shit, shit shit. Why didn't they leave the children alone," he shouted at the wall. The echo of his voice brought back his own loss as a child in Detroit.

DETROIT

Young Mike sat patiently as the trip into Detroit took over an hour in the old Model T Ford. They were going to visit Scotty Strachan and his family. He liked Scotty and the way he would roar out with a Scottish accent as though he were indeed as fierce as he looked. And sometimes he would rotate the false teeth he wore sideways in his mouth which always set the boys awash in uncontrollable laughter. Their son Robbie was Michael's age and the two were close friends.

It was a cold trip as the heater in the old Ford was one of the first and not very reliable. They arrived safely, greetings were passed all around, Pete and his mother joined the Strachans for a drink while Michael and Robbie went off to play. Soon dinner was ready and after they ate the boys went back to playing in Robbie's room for a few hours.

"Michael," his mother called. This time her voice was a little higher pitched since he hadn't responded the first time. They were playing Chinese checkers. "I'm in here with Robbie," he answered reluctantly knowing he would have to go.

"It's time to leave and we have a long drive ahead of us," said his mother as she came down the carpeted hallway into

Robby's bedroom. "It's Christmas Eve. You'll be up early in the morning to open your presents".

It was time to launch their plan. "Mom, can I stay here tonight with Robbie?" He pleaded. "They are coming out tomorrow for Christmas dinner and I can come out with them." He looked expectantly at Robbie who joined in.

"Yes, Mrs. Trout, he could come out with us. Please!"

His mother looked down at him, the worry lines around her eyes crinkling with a smile. "Are you sure you don't want to be home to open your presents tonight?" She asked.

"It will just be more fun here with Robbie," he replied. "I have no one to play with at home."

All right," she agreed. "Come give me a hug and we'll be on our way." He gave her the hug and a kiss that resounded around the room. She clung to him as he tried to pull away and pulled him back for a second kiss then left...for good

Morning came. The boys chattered excitedly as Robbie opened his presents. His parents had seen to it there were two for Michael. Breakfast consisted of plates of hot pancakes with butter melting in rivulets of succulence down the sides topped by pure maple syrup; Scotty would have none of the "sugar water stuff." The aroma of fresh coffee interlaced with the sizzling of sausages wrapped around the warm kitchen like a soft blanket of contentment. Large quantities of the sweet cakes slid down young throats and filled the souls as well at the stomachs.

When it was time to depart they climbed into Scotty's old Desoto and settled down for the long drive to Taylor, Michigan. The boys played Chinese checkers while the Strockans discussed the Joe Louis fight that was to take place soon at the Olympia Stadium on Grand River Avenue. As they talked their breaths made ice fogs that settled on the windows as a frost; the heater in their old workhorse wasn't very efficient either. Michael was explaining for the fourth time all the presents he had under his tree when his house came into view just down the left side of the dirt road.

Michael started to open the car door to jump out when Scotty said ominously, "Just a minute Michael." They sat looking at the tiny house. There was no smoke coming out of the chimney, the hand pump outside was covered with snow and Pete's car was not in the driveway. There were no lights in the house even though it was an overcast and somewhat dark day. Michael, attempting to see out the windows, became uncomfortable. It was eerily quiet as snow began to fall silently to cover any warmth with a white blanket stifling all sound, all feeling.

"There's no car here in the yard," Robbie's mother said as she drew in a sharp breath as though her chest had tightened. "Pete must be in town," replied Scotty.

"It's so quiet," she said as Michael opened his door and ran up the dirt walkway and burst into the house. "It's so quiet and…

"Mom," yelled Michael as he stood still in the cold, quiet kitchen looking through the narrow doorway into the living room. He could see the tree they had decorated the day before and the presents but that was all. An eager young boy who filled the room with his excitement had placed the presents underneath to undergo constant re-arrangement. His mother and stepfather slept in the little bedroom off this room and he looked in but there was no one there and nothing moved in the frigid air.

"Mom," he said softly turning his head expectantly, knowing that she would come into the room at any minute as she always did when he called, she had to. "Mom!" he repeated over and over as he walked into the front room. The gifts lay untouched. No fire had been started. No living thing had been here for a long time.

"Mom!" his voice quavered. He looked from the cold stove to the tree then into the bedroom willing his mother to walk through the door. "Mother, where are you?" he wailed. Where was the one constant thing in his life? "Motherrrrrrrrrr…" He sank to his knees as if to pray her presence. The Strockans stood together watching him, listening to his pain as his frozen words careened off the walls in mournful echoes. Tears streamed down Ester Strochan's face as she clutched her boy to her. She knew, she just knew tragedy lived in this tiny house this day.

He felt a heavy hand on his shoulder. "Michael," it was Scotty's voice. "There's been an accident," he said gently. Michael looked up into a face filled with grief. "I found a note on the door from the state police and we have to call them,"

"Is my mom all right?" asked the boy. "Is she O.K.?"

"I'm sure she is fine," replied Scotty as he went to the far end of the kitchen to make the call. "Can you fix a fire?"

"Sure," replied Michael as he busied himself crumpling up newspaper, placing it in the stove, lighting it, and then placing a paper wrapped briquette of coal on top to catch. Someone, for some reason, had shattered his Christmas Day and it lay all around him in icy pieces.

Scotty called his wife into the kitchen where Michael could not hear. He related the results of the phone call. Michael's mother was dead, killed by a drunken soldier last night. She had been sitting where Michael would have been; the "Suicide Seat" they called it since so many passengers were killed and not the driver. His stepfather was injured slightly and in the hospital.

Mike was alone now.

THE TRAIN RIDE

Young Mike sat there rocking back forth with the motion of the train. Lonely, sixteen years old, he should have been playing hockey in someone's back yard. It was December 31, 1941 and very cold outside. The clickety-clack of the wheels rumbled up through the floor of the car which was empty except for him. His coat jacket kept him warm but he could see his breath in the frosty air. He shivered repeatedly as the snow covered landscape flashed by. It wasn't so much the snow as the winter in his young soul. Every so often his face would scrunch up in pain and tears would leak from his eyes running in rivulets down his cheeks until he got control again. He stared out the window into the countryside flashing by as if trying to see reasons why this had happened to him.

He was going over the recent past not quite understanding what had occurred in his young life. His eyes fixed on a small back door ahead on a home similar to the one he had shared with his mother. The past gently nudged the present aside as he remembered; her smell of lavender; the softness of her hands when she rubbed his chest with Vicks Vapo Rub to ease a cold; the gentle chiding when he sloshed the water from the pan under the icebox trying to empty it without spilling. The train's whistle shrieked him back to reality as it sped towards

Tuscola, Illinois where his mother was to be buried. He was to meet his biological father for the first time. So much tragedy for so young a boy.

Rising he walked to the door of the car. As he opened it the crescendo of the steel wheels on the frozen tracks flew up at him and the icy wind tugged at his jacket. Getting the door to the next car open was difficult. He wobbled through several cars containing just a few other passengers, all with heads leaning against backs of the wicker seats, resting fitfully. He came to the baggage car. Entering he saw the casket with his mother's body, swaying back and forth on an ocean of frosty air. Tiptoeing over to it so as if to not disturb her he rested his hand on it ever so gently

Suddenly, out of the chilly air came a voice, "That yours young fella?" the baggage car man asked dispassionately. He was sitting by a small coal stove dressed in a heavy wool coat with his head covered by a hat from which earmuffs covered his ears and was tied by a string beneath his chin.

"Yes sir," he replied. "It's my mother."

"Sorry to hear it," he responded gently as he rose and wandered to the rear of the car, then out the door so as to provide privacy in this moment of sorrow.

They were together. He and his mom. For the last time. The dim bulb barely illuminated his small body and the casket in a yellow hue. The train whistle mourned through the night for him as he stood there silently, hand resting on the casket as though to touch her, sobbing silently.

"Mom," he whispered.

MARCO

His thin, six foot frame draped the bar at club 720 on Wells street this muggy afternoon. It was the standard watering hole with a juke box up against one wall, pictures of sports jocks on the opposite wall and the ever-present odor of stale beer and cigarette smoke. With his glass of tequila resting between his forearms he reached up to stroke the large black mustache he was so proud of and smiled as his fingers touched bare skin; the police report on the evening news had described it as a means of identification. He had left the "Irish Travelers" right after he and his cohorts killed the family that was so close to Mike.

Lanky, good looking in a swarthy way with hair slicked back, he had the look of a Don Juan. His eyes masked cruelty and never looked right at you as though he were afraid you would see his evil. He always wore the "Cuba" boots, the ones with narrow toes and built up heels. Preferring black his clothes fit tight on a muscular frame; his pant legs tapered. Never without his gold neck chain he was an attractive hombre. His constant companion was what he called El Rostillo; he carried a straight razor at all times. The front door banged open letting in a puff of moist air and a lovely blonde.

Sharon swept in and headed for the ladies room, late as usual for her job. As she struggled with a large garment bag he recognized her as a fashion show worker; one of those would-be models about to display her body in "baby dolls" and anything else filmy enough to titillate the bar patrons. The owner felt it brought in customers and the woman was paid for doing something she enjoyed. She could claim to be a model at $7.00 an hour for two hours. She was allowed to keep the money from whatever was bought from her.

It was a pain lugging that weight around on a rainy day like today. And trying to change in a cramped bathroom was the bane of her existence. The floors were dirty and there were never enough places to hang things. Any request to the management only brought a grope for her breasts and a suggestion she "put out," Marco watched as she emerged in a sheer "shortie" revealing a posterior that was full and jiggly on top of what he thought of as "chicken legs" those meaty thighs followed by very long slim limbs. She aroused in him a dangerous longing he first sensed as a young boy looking at movie magazines left by the "Gringos" in his village. Marilyn Monroe had captivated him. Many times he played with himself as he stared at her picture; a friend had shown him how to use Vaseline when he made a fist.

Once she looked up into his baleful stare and shivered feeling as though an animal was tracking her. She wasn't all that wrong. This Latino Jeffrey Dahmer had taken flesh from a female victim to not only be in her but to have some of her in him; all the more to vanquish her. This young woman was in trouble, serious trouble. The man next to him was also Latino and asked "Where ya from?" trying to start a conversation. Marcos looked at him sideways deciding whether or not he wanted to talk to the man.

"I'm from the "Mixteca from the state of Puebla. Y Usted?"

"Second generation amigo," replied the man. "You're from the poor southern half of Mexico if I know my map and people; a Mestizo."

Marcos's eyes followed her around the room; he was a shark circling its prey. He wasn't comfortable with people who asked questions and this Porcho was no exception. "I was raised in Chinanatla. I hacked weeds in the cornfields and hawked soda pop and chewing gum in the plaza for money." His father had been a drunk that beat him almost daily. His mother ceased to care long ago and took what comfort she could find at the church.

"They have a big church in that town don't they?" offered his new companion. "They always waste the peon's money on churches and vestments while the people go hungry and uneducated. How come you left?"

"The work went away with modernization and the church held nothing for me. Many priests have housekeepers they bed or children they molest as he had been molested. It's a joke in the villages." He had learned deceit and violence from the church. Even the wall in the hut where he was raised had a picture of a huge heart with large blood drops spattering out of it as the "blood of Jesus." A picture heralding his ancestors, the Aztecs, and their penchant for human sacrifice hung next to it. He had found it in the plaza and in his village if you found something you took it. He learned to enjoy the power of slaughtering pigs. Many times he had raped eight and ten year old little girls not for love, for power. He was an angry man from an angry society that lay festering for thousands of years while America ran past them in less than half a century.

"Things would not be so bad if the gringos hadn't stolen Texas and California."

"Yeah." scoffed his companion, "They should have left them alone. Then they could be poor and barren just like Mexico."

Marcos had been brought over as a "Puros Poblanos," or "pure peasant" by a man who needed workers for his Tortilleria, a business that catered to the addicts needing their tortilla fix. Each weekend a line formed early outside of "Piaxtal, Buena Vista or Chinatla", the "Tortilla Triangle" patiently waiting to get their fresh corn products resembling a pancake. He worked hard helping to make 400,000 tortillas a week for the growing Mexican population in the New York area. His boss, a Mexican himself, was fair and paid good wages.

The only place he could afford to live was in the "Burning Bronx" where he suffered the indignities perpetrated on him by his own kind. His hardship continued in "The Well", an area in Brooklyn so named for the degradation suffered by the drug users. From here he went into the more insidious hell of the South Bronx and often got caught in the gang wars of the "Savage Skulls." He was once dangled out the window of a sixth floor apartment until he agreed to perform fellatio on one of the gang members. This experience made him decide to come to Chicago where he had heard the Mexican population would soon be a majority and one-day run the city. "You working?" he asked.

"Sure, over at the aquarium. Come on over if you're lookin' for work. Ask for me Miguel, Miggy for short. I'll give you an intro to the head honcho."

"Nah, I'm workin' for a group they call 'Irish Travelers.' They work neighborhoods doin odd jobs and the like. We make good money scammin' people, especially old people. They work out of South Carolina somewhere. Heard about them out east. Heard they make up to $50,000.00 a year." He never took his eyes off Sharon who was laughing with one of the customers. She sold him a raffle ticket for a baby doll then moved to the next table.

The jiggling curves of her buttocks drove him a little crazy. He had to have that bitch. It was time to tap a kidney; he looked up, saw the men's room sign and headed that way. It was down a little hallway and separated from the bar area by a short wall on top of which sat a curtain of dowels giving it the appearance of a cage. He stood behind it rubbing his fly area and staring at her, getting harder as he stared. Spontaneously she looked up and to the side staring right into his face, a lion staring through the bars of a cage at a victim. "Oh Shit," she said softly feeling a band of fear around her heart; she recognized a predator when she saw one. His leer would scare Saint Michael it was that foreboding. Walking slowly he kept staring as he passed out of view.

Entering the toilet area he came across a man standing up against one of the doors. He stood watching and could tell from the noises there was someone on the other side of the door. The man had gripped the top of the door with both hands and was groaning. "Yea baby," he yelled his hips moving in and out against the door, "Take it all baby, oh Christ yea," he was in a spasm. Suddenly he was quiet and as Marcos watched pulled back so he could see an erection come out of a hole in the door. The door opened and an effeminate looking guy came out looking mad as hell and also holding his penis in his hand.

"God dam it you didn't wait for me you greedy, lying bastard," he yelled at the guy who had been at the door. He kept ranting as Marcos went up to the urinal to relieve himself. Someone had thrown a cigarette in the bowl and he concentrated on pissing it to shreds. He knew what he had just seen. The door had a hole in it called the "Glory Hole." One man gets behind the door and the other guy pushes his erection through. This first guy masturbates as he performs fellatio and the arrangement is to wait until both are ready. "She" as he would be known among the Gays was still yelling, "You got no right to treat me this way, I'm in show business."

"Yeah," sneered0 the other guy, "Some show business." He looked over at Marcos and said, "He's a Fluffer, you know, he sucks guys so they can get hard and have sex in porn movies. He fluffs 'em up for the camera." Marcos shrugged and left the room. Sharon had decided to avoid him and went back to the other side of the bar. He motioned to the bartender he wanted her down his way. "Hey honey," the bartender growled, "Come over here and see this nice man." You didn't ignore this guy; he was rough on the girls. She came around the bar and stood in front of Marcos. "Like this?" She teased leaning forward and down so her breasts almost covered his face. Her smell of Jasmine reached down to his groin.

"I like it just fine," he replied looking down the cleavage at the front at two generous white breasts with no bra. She was of solid flesh and he could almost taste her nipples.

"Your lady would like it too. I'll bet if you took this home you would be treated special tonight," looking sideways and dropping her eyes he thought of a movie he saw once on the side of a building in the village. She looked and talked like the actress Mae West. She moved closer to him.

"No thanks," he said "but I will buy a raffle ticket."

"That's two dollars,' she quipped taking the money and handing him the ticket. Just then one of the drunks grabbed at her. She was experienced but this one wouldn't stop pawing at her breasts. When she pulled away and he went after her Marcos pulled the straight razor from its sheath under his shirt. "Leave the woman alone," he threatened holding the blade between his thumb and forefinger with the back part over the back of his hand with it hidden behind his back.

"Back off spick," yelled a big man coming alongside. He was apparently a buddy of the drunk or just didn't like Latinos. "Back off or I'll nail ya." He followed up with a punch thrown at his head. Marcos pulled back smoothly, like a cat, letting the fist fan his nose. At the same time his hand swept up and down the man's arm which went crimson but he didn't notice. When cut with a straight razor there is no immediate feeling. Now the guy lunged trying to grab his throat. He deftly went under the arms spun around and was behind him. Once again he swung his arm in an arc. This time the white shirt exploded with crimson and a second cut for formed an "x". The bartender came around the bar with a baseball bat heading right for Marcos.

"You better get out of here amigo," urged Miggy "or the cops are gonna be all over you like flies on a pile of shit."

In one move Marcos closed the razor, returned it to his shirt and took his change off the bar. He was out the door in less than a minute while the bartender yelled for someone to call 911. He found his car and drove around for an hour then returned so that he could watch the front door. He sat there fantasizing about the girl and what he would do with her, rubbing his crotch in anticipation. That he would have this woman there was no doubt, it was simply a case of when and where.

THE STALKER

Sharon came out of the bar with the heavy bag clasped in her arms and struggled down the street to her car. Marcos hurried to come up behind her. "Here Miss, let me help you," he offered while taking the bag out of her hands. She protested a little, swept a loose lock of hair out of her face, then graciously accepted his help. Reaching a small red Pinto wagon with rusted fenders she used her key and opened the back hatch. He placed the bag inside for her and noticed a nurse's cap neatly placed in a box that had the letters "Sherman Hospital Elgin, Illinois" written on it. He closed the lid.

"You should be careful in these areas," he offered helpfully, "there are some bad people around here. Do you have far to go?" He had a friendly smile with white teeth that disarmed more than one female.

She stared at him for a moment then released her guard enough to smile and reply "Not too far thank you," her lips were full and soft looking. She had a way of looking at men from the side that invited them to try a little harder, which she really didn't want at this time but couldn't help. It was a "Why don't you come up and see me sometime" smile that rivaled anything Mae West had put on the silver screen. Sharon had a need to titillate men, all men, it was in her nature. She bent to enter her vehicle. He looked down the top of her dress at full breasts that strengthened his resolve to have her.

"I don't suppose you would be interested in dinner sometime?' he suggested.

"No thanks not this time," she teased knowing he would get the suggestion that he ask again and put and end to it by shutting the door and starting the engine. She dangled men this way all the time. He hurried back to his car and followed her at a discrete distance. He was good; he had done this many times before. He would let her get two blocks ahead. If she turned he would turn in the same direction one block before, pacing so that he could see her pass the intersection a block to his right. Periodically he would place himself directly behind her. She took Ohio Street to the Kennedy Expressway and headed towards O'Hare field. Following her was a snap. She paid one toll then proceeded to the Elgin exit. Marcos thought to himself that this was one long trip to make for a two-hour job. "This broad doesn't know how to figure expenses," he said out loud.

At Elgin she took off onto route 25, turned south proceeding to route 20 which she took west to the little town of Udina. Here she turned into the gravel driveway of a small white house; parked, tugged the clothing bag until it came out then carried it inside. Marcos drove past feeling a surge of sexual arousal at how easy this was going to be. Making two right turns he was in front of an abandoned store, its windows boarded up. Parking behind it his car was hidden from view and he could see into her kitchen. Using powerful binoculars he located each room then fixed on the shadow moving behind the small, frosted bathroom window.

Sharon Parsons was married when she became pregnant at fifteen years of age and wound up with two children by the time she was 17. Working hard and helped by her husband who worked for AT&T she got through nurse's school and hired in at Sherman Hospital. She supplemented her income and fed her ego at the same time by modeling in bars.

She was many things including a good mother but her passionate nature got her in trouble even when she was in school; she seduced the English teacher, Mr Scorzy, in his office. He was of average height, had a full head of black hair and kept his mustache neatly trimmed. His clothing though dated was always well coordinated and at times he managed to look rather dapper. All the other girls kidded about the bulge in his trousers and Sharon decided to have a look at it to check out the rumors

Sitting in the front row she managed to hike her skirt up so he could see between her legs. This coupled with the tight sweater she wore would have seduced Saint Peter. He asked her to stay after class one day and closed the door when she came into his office. Sharon made her willingness clear when she pulled down the shade covering the glass window in the door. This poor man, helpless now with desire, reached out to embrace her. They kissed passionately and he wasn't too bad at it. Sharon sank down, unzipped his trousers, pulled them down along with his Jockey shorts and found to her delight that he was rather generous. She heard him gasp when she took him. She had him, he was completely in her control his body shaking uncontrollably and he surrendered everything.

Rising, she undid her bra which opened from the front, and pulled his face into her full breasts. Taking the other in his hand he nursed like a newborn. Sharon pressed back against the wall moaning, pulling his head into her. Suddenly, spasmodically, the back of her head pressed harder against the wall, she trembled uncontrollably again and again for a full minute. One after another they rolled over her. Then it was done. Pushing him away she did up her bra, straightened her skirt and left the room not even looking back at the bewildered face. She did hear him stammering something about "When" and "Again" but she didn't stop. It was over until she decided when the next time would be, if ever. From this she learned about herself and her needs and took every opportunity that presented itself to satisfy them.

Sharon preferred to make oral love to men; it was a compulsion and the more they gave the better. She would instruct them to fondle and suck her breasts as this brought her to orgasm every time. Having seen the picture Deep Throat she wondered if her clitoris was in her breasts. At this time of her life she loved her husband but suffered a compulsion to have many men in addition to him. The lunchtime modeling job was ideal for the pursuit of this need.

That evening after dinner the baby sitter had allowed the children to play outside until dark. Sharon used her when her husband was out of town at a training seminar. Entering the house she greeted her, got details on the children, paid her and went in to see them. Patty, her seven-year-old, had a new bruise, which she kissed and made all better. With a pat on the behind she was off to bed. Darlene was laying in the small sitting room on the floor her chin resting in her hands. Since she was ten she was allowed a half-hour longer.

"Why are you way in there honey," she asked, "The TV is so far from you. Why don't you move closer into the room? You could see better. Why are you so far from the TV?"

"Cause," replied the precocious little nymph, "This is the scary part." Sharon studied her for a moment then suddenly realized the sense of such reasoning to a ten-year-old. When it gets scary you move away from it even if it is only on television. 'Wish life was really that simple' she thought. Busying herself straightening up the front room she had little else on her mind than lounging in a hot tube with her favorite CD romancing her. There were shoes and stockings to put in the hamper; little blue jeans to fold and place in drawers and toys to collect. Midway she ordered the television turned off and a kiss before the tucking in. Darlene wasn't too happy about it but her yawn indicated the order came none too soon. She kissed her mom and left to crawl into bed. It took another half-hour to lay out the kid's clothes for the next day and then she felt she could collapse.

Her bathroom was her haven. Candles were her favorite light source and they cast flickering shadows on the walls. The motif was Orchid colorations on the towels and wash cloths. The soap dispenser was Purple, the dish it sat on light green. She carried the scheme through with pastel shower curtains pulled back, held in place by soft, beige clasps. Having filled the tub she lay in the refreshingly steamy aroma of Romantic Rose bath bubbles.

As she soaked Marcos had left his car and was slithering through two yards to approach the house. He stood quietly rubbing himself as he anticipated his moves. He had spent half an hour looking over the area, plotting a quick escape route should one be needed.

A short time later Sharon lay in her bathrobe watching the 10 o'clock news not hearing the back door open. He had used a credit card to slide into the door crack and open the old lock. Marcos stood in the darkened kitchen listening to the clock. Part of the enjoyment of a predator was the visualization of the act. The feeling the old priest had warned him about in the village rose in his lower body.

DOMINATION

Moving quickly he wrapped one arm around her, holding up his razor for her to see. "No sound," he whispered, "or you'll end up like the guy in the bar. She froze.

"Don't hurt my kids," she pleaded. "Please don't hurt the children."

"I have no intention of hurting anybody," he lied. He pulled her to her feet, turned her to face him and turned out the floor lamp but kept light in the room by leaving the television on hitting the Mute button on the control. Opening the sash to her robe he exposed two beautifully formed breasts. She let the robe fall to the floor. Dropping to his knees he began nursing.

In spite of her fear she lay back her head dreamily and said softly "Oh you're good, you are so good," he nibbled one while his left hand massaged the other. Her skin was soft with the odor of perfumed soap. He knew just where to stroke and what to squeeze. He felt her nipple grow turgid under his urging. He took large portions of each breast in his mouth to bite causing her to whimper but she didn't ask him to stop. Suddenly she pulled his head into her breast as her body shook as she moaned loudly. 'Christ,' he thought, 'This bitch is having an orgasm.' When she stopped trembling she pulled him upright, sank to her knees to undo his pants zipper. She took him out remarking, "My, aren't we a big boy." She stroked the length occasionally taking the head into her cupped palm to rub it in the increasing moistness that emitted. Round and round she moved her hand then suddenly took him. He exploded and she took him in again. The raper had become the raped.

Marcos didn't like the loss of control. Pulling her up he threw her over the back of the stuffed chair and drove into her. She cried out but her large, soft cheeks drove him crazy. The more she whimpered the harder he drove. All his angers were unleashed. He would consume this bitch any way he wanted. The tightness, the softness of her cheeks made him delirious. Suddenly she reached between her legs grabbing his testicles her nails digging into the soft tissue and now she was crying loudly. He lost it. He turned her around and smashed a fist into the side of her head driving her senseless. Out came his straight razor that gleamed as he opened the blade. "I'm gonna slice you like the pig you are," he muttered. He lowered it to cut when but hesitated at a yell from one of the bedrooms. Letting her fall to the floor he headed down the hall to the sound of the noise.

It was a narrow hallway and he could see one bedroom illuminated by a night-light where the door was ajar. Pushing the door further open he could see the little ten year old girl lying on top of the covers talking in her dream. Her gown was up around her hips exposing a bare soft, white posterior. Marcos stared at her bottom. He couldn't take his eyes off her. Feeling himself start to harden and enlarge again he walked silently towards the bed unzipping his trousers relishing how he would savage the helpless little victim.

A FRIEND IN NEED

Mike, standing in front of the south wall of his dining room, placed his hand over an oval picture of his grandmother, resting his thumb on her brooch which was a print reader. As he did so a laser scanned his iris. He spoke, "nemesis" to give a voice print and a section of the wall recessed then slid aside so that he could enter; this was Biometrics at work. The door slid shut.

He sat at the center of a wide semicircular desk and looked at the wall in front of him. In the center were four 27-inch, flat TFT television screens flanked on all sides by 10-inch screens. He could view individual pictures or phase-lock them together to have one massive view of whatever came over the satellite. The master control board was blinking LED's of yellow, red and green color. Currently on the screen was a view of his property from all angles. He spoke, "Lights" and the room went dark.

He sat in the totally darkened study with his microphone/headset on and a voice-actuated software booted up and ready. Every 30 seconds a sound would come from the studio-grade tape recorder, a gift from his old friend Bernie Clapper who had been president of Universal Recording Studios, one of Chicago's most prestigious recording companies. Sounds such as a knife being removed from its scabbard, a gun being cocked, the virtually non-existent noise of rubber soled shoes sneaking along, a man or a woman breathing so as not to be heard, a rope thrown over a wall and all sounds that might be encountered on a clandestine operation were randomly emitted.. At each sound he would speak into the headset microphone saying what he thought the sound was. Later, when he turned the lights on he would see two rows of data. The first delineated what the noise was, the second his verbalization. In this manner he kept sharp the skills that had carried him though so many challenging times.

Never forgetting the importance of night vision Mike spent at least 20 minutes each day, in the dark, practicing visual acuity. Knowing the macula, the area surrounding the pupil of the eye, carried 120 million cones he practiced looking at items by not looking directly at them: he looked at them from the corners of his eyes where the cones were most sensitive to light. This exercise permitted him to see things others could never discern and had kept him alive many times at night in the jungle. Later on he would practice assembling various handguns and automatic weapons in the dark always moving to decrease the time it took him to acquire a working weapon.

In concert with visual acuity his RISC based computer controlled a tiny compressor that periodically emitted odors such as cigarette and pipe smoke to identify which brand, perfumes, exhaust from various cars as well as odors taken from the clothing of various men and women. As he smelled each one he would verbally identify it and the computer gave him a printout of his verbal identification and the actual definition of the odor. Suddenly one of his alarms set off a soft, high-pitched signal.

His computer screen had laid out a grid of his property. Sensors around the perimeter and spaced throughout the area provided information about who or what was approaching and from which direction. A cursor blinked along the course of the driveway. Atop the screen were calculations that identified it as an automobile by its speed and weight. Had it been a rabbit running across the open field it would have been so noted. Hitting the "print screen" button he brought the video camera into play and saw it was his marine buddy Jack Toneg coming up the driveway.

He cleared all circuits, opened the north garage door as well as the door in the wall and continued his exercises; he had decided to let Jack see what he had. It wasn't long before he appeared in the room his mustache moving up and down as he chewed gum. Mike noticed his stomach was hanging a little farther over his belt, due no doubt to his propensity for sweet rolls. He wore his usual confused look as he watched Mike for a minute then said, "This is awesome good buddy, what is all that you do? I know it isn't my concern but I've always been curious. For an example, I saw the garage door going up as I approached, how did you know I was coming?"

Mike swept his arm in an arc as he said "The periphery of my land is imbedded with solar powered sensors. I use WiFi techniques for transmission. They are spaced precisely to sense the approach of anything from any direction. My computers evaluate and with sub-routines can calculate weight, direction and speed. Once they have that the proper alert is given and whatever it is comes on camera

"And what camera?" Jack asked confused. "I know a video camera when I see one and I have never seen one around here."

"That's because all of the floodlights you see on the house and sheds have built in video cams feeding into the control panel".

"Man, you have more dam gear and things going on. I don't want to go where I'm not wanted but just what are you doing now?"

"That's OK my friend, I don't mind telling you" Mike answered. "I have the Dragon Naturally Speaking voice response software running. Listen closely and you will hear sounds spaced 30 seconds apart from this tape recorder. Various sounds will emanate which I identify. Jack had leaned forward in interest. "I'll be dammed", he muttered, "Outstanding."

"I also spend time perfecting my night vision," Mike continued, The eye is surrounded with rods that are more sensitive than any other part so I practice looking at things, in the dark, out of the corner of my eye. Later I practice assembling various handguns and automatic weapons in the dark always moving to decrease the time it takes me to acquire a working piece."

"Dam man, you are a piece of work," Jack responded with respect. "You are one dangerous dude."

"I also work on my abilities to identify different smells. When you detect an odor it comes in the form of molecules which are detected by a mucous membrane tissue. This tissue is covered with receptor cells mounted on microscopic hairs sticking out and waving in the air currents as we inhale.. The olfactory bulb, located above the nasal cavity sends data to the limbic system in the brain and you determine the origin." The look on Jack's face told him his words had meant nothing to this good natured friend

"And what were you saying one day about a tomahawk and them things they show the Ninjas' throwing in the movies?" Jack asked..

"I did use what I called a Combat Tomahawk on the islands. I perfected my ability to throw it accurately and the Corps let me keep it. It's a great way to take out a sentry silently if you know how. As to the things the Ninjas use in the movies those are called Shurikens or "throwing stars. They fall into a class called *Tonki* by the Japanese. By themselves they would at best make the victim uncomfortable. I have to laugh in a movie when they showed someone dying with one protruding from his head. Their construction is such the point could penetrate but an inch into the body and do little more than distract a guy for a minute. He stood up and motioned his friend to follow him.

In the basement he had set up a computer controlled mechanism whereby a plywood outline of a man would be located in various positions by moving silently on a track. Telling Jack to stand over by a wall he turned on the system. With his back turned to it he heard a note, spun around with a Shuriken in his hand having to decide instantaneously as to target location vertically and horizontally then hurled it underhanded and sideways. It whistled through the aid and landed in the neck of the figure.

Jack slapped his forehead in disbelief. "Outstanding. Man you gotta show me how to do that, you just gotta!" He thought for a minute then said, "But if it's like you say that it can only irritate a guy then are they of any use?"

Mike held one up for Jack to see. "I have devised a design whereby they are thicker consisting of two separate pieces welded together with a space in-between for fluid. There is a sharp needle in each point behind a diaphragm which holds fluid in the chamber. Upon hitting its target the needle moves forward, penetrates the diaphragm causing the fluid to squirt into the victim. In some of them the liquid is lethal causing instant death. In others it is Adenosine, a chemical found in the brains of cats that are napping that cause them to fall into a deep slumber. A friend who was a research scientist at Northwestern University and went through about 20 cats a week provided me with this fluid."

"Like I said Mike, you are a piece of work and that confuses the hell outta me. You're a vegetarian and yet one dangerous son-of-a-bitch.

"You're not thinking Jack. I'm only dangerous if you attack me or mine. What is the biggest, strongest and most dangerous animal in the world; the king of the jungle?

"The lion?" Jack said.

"That's the stupid data put out by Hollywood. Keep in mind Hollywood was begun by a bunch of European Jews who knew nothing about the realities of the life in the jungle. The elephant is the king of the jungle. An elephant will kill a lion ever time as will a hippo. And what is the elephant?" Mike quizzed.

Jack shrugged, "A vegetarian I guess."

"And the meanest is the Rhinoceros, the most dangerous the Water Buffalo and the beast that kills more humans than anything else is the Hippopotamus: all vegetarians. You attack or encroach on the property of any of them and you have one hell of a fight on your hands.

All of the long-living animals are vegetarians. The lions and tigers, the predators are garbage eaters. They go after the sick, the lame, the old. Hell they even eat the lion cubs of others. They are cowards every one of them. By eating the flesh of the sick they become sick and have an average life span of only five years. All of us have the ability and desire to protect ourselves against the predators." Mike turned to look Jack squarely in the face. "And never forget, the vegetarians can survive without the predators but the predators cannot survive without the vegetarians. Do you remember those two teen-aged girls that were kidnapped a few years ago? They stabbed their captor with a bottle they had broken and cut his throat so they could escape. And, by God, they did escape."

"Seems to me I do," responded Jack.

"How many people teach their children, girls especially, to fight back if they are abducted?" Mike words were clipped now and his face had an angry glow. "How many would instruct the girls to find a weapon and kill the kidnapper? How many do you think, Jack?" He turned and glared out the window. "None, that's how many. So what do they do? They pray and cry and that delights the sonofabitch who's nabbed them. Pray my ass, you better teach them survival first. I have yet to see anyone saved by prayer."

"What about these stories you hear about the healing power of prayer? What about the people who say they were saved by prayer?" Jack asked timidly, drawing on his somewhat fundamentalist background. "Do you think they lie or invent things?"

"You bet I do," Mike flashed back. "If they are saved from a bad situation it was because someone else worked while they prayed. There are many children who would be alive today if they had been taught the fundamentals of making a weapon and killing a captor. It breaks my heart sometimes to see the carnage of our children due to lack of education." Mike kicked a chair. "It is lack of education that made prey out of children to pedophile priests. And the movies are partly at fault also because they always show the dimwitted kid praying instead of taking action so that's why the people who watch often them do nothing!"

"Well all I can say is I'd be in your platoon any day. Having said that I'm outta here, I've got to get home and mow the lawn". Mike knew this friend had something on his mind because he remained seated looking a little forlorn.

"Jack are you OK?" Mike asked. "You look a bit weather-beaten and tired. You got something I can help you with old friend?"

Jack's face had crumbled around his mouth like boulders around an abandoned mine shaft. His eyes were misty. He looked down at his interlocked fingers for a moment then over at Mike for a full minute before he spoke again. "I got scared an hour ago and I need someone to talk to."

TUTELARIES

It has often been said that over each of us lingers a guardian angel, a 'Tinker Bell' type of creature that sees to our well being. Some, such as Honorius of Autun referred to them as "Tutelary Spirits" to which Thomas Aquinas was in agreement. Saint Gemma Galgani insists she had spoken with hers. Darlene's must have been hard at work this night. This innocent little girl would not be violated; not in this town, not in this house, not on this night.

He stood there, his erection demanding satisfaction, savoring those little white cheeks. He imagined how it would be when he began kissing then nibbling them, he seemed to grow even larger. The little one turned one her side and he reached out to turn her on her stomach again. All of a sudden he jerked and stared out the window as the walls of the quiet room exploded with red, blue and white flashes from a police car. Marcos moved over to the window and saw two uniformed officers talking to a woman down the block; she was pointing the the back yard area he had travelled. Silently he left the room entering the kitchen to leave through the back door. As an afterthought he took the top off a cookie jar sitting on the counter and pulled out a small roll of bills that he thought might be there. He oozed silently into the night taking one of the routes he had laid out.

Later when he unrolled the bills he also found a picture of a beautiful girl with her address and an invitation to visit on the back. It was of Leslie.

JACK IN A BOX

"Let's go upstairs," said Mike leading the way. When in the living room Mike sat down, leaned back with a look of dedicated interest in his eyes that invited Jack to continue.

"You know I'm an alcoholic but you don't know much more," Jack began. "The truth is I used my experience as a prisoner of war to launch a stupid-assed drinking career. It cost me my marriage, my health and my dignity. When I woke up one morning in a ditch with nothing but my skivvies on I knew I was either going to change or die. I mean goddam it Mike when some kids can beat you up and steal your clothes you know it's over." He glanced at Mike expecting a response, none came so he continued. "By this time I had no credentials that would allow me to join any group. I was a constant drunk, always sick at heart with disgust that only an alcoholic can understand. I had nothing; no address, no telephone, no religion, no job, no references."

"References," he repeated sarcastically, "Any of my past employers would have warned others to bar the doors against me." He looked up at Mike his eyes moist now. "Hell Mike, I couldn't afford to enter a penny arcade. I was dirty, I stank and my behavior all that time certainly did not rate any kindness.

Then I heard of Alcoholics Anonymous, looked it up in the Yellow Pages and went to the address of the nearest one ." Jack took a moment to compose himself.

"When I thought of going in I thought 'Hell all I got for them is a sickness to offer.' It turns out that is all they asked of me. When I walked up the steps of the old AA clubhouse on New York's West 41st Street I was essentially a dead man. I was so numb that even without a coat I was oblivious to the bitter January weather. The shaking I couldn't control I pretended was deliberate. As I walked in I knew that I must hold on for one more minute, force my legs to take one more step, try to think of some great happy moment in the past, (or invent one), and sooner or later I could get a drink or simply fall on the floor and die. I had no strength to ask for help. I felt I was taking a risk getting near strangers who, I was told, did not ask for names and had been pretty bad drinkers themselves, just to see whether I could observe while being unobserved." He was wringing the fingers of his left hand now with his right, squeezing hard as if to press out the pain.

"I was prepared with lies; ask me how much I drank and I lied. If someone were to ask me what I would do to get a drink I would lie fearing the truth would result in punishment.

If they asked how I behaved when drinking I would lie to cover the blackouts and the shameful parts I was able to remember. It turns out none of this mattered as the lady who first talked to me had only one thing, compassion.

The agony being experienced by this old friend began to get to Mike. He stood up, shuffled uneasily towards Jack, changed his mind and sat back down again. "What happened then Jack?" he asked.

Turning he said, "I stood in front of a bulletin board pretending to read and saw her standing there looking at me. I figured she was with the group and waited for her to ask me some dumb question or make a stupid declaration." He turned at looked directly at Mike now. "She did not."

"What I needed desperately at that moment was a stiff drink," Jack continued softly, "which I would have been too afraid to take even if she had offered it to me. Then suddenly, through my alcoholic haze, through the fog of self-hate, I heard this gentle voice say quietly, "Are you having trouble with your drinking? He looked at Mike beseechingly while a tear ran down his right cheek. He choked up then sat down tears streaming now like a torrent of pain sweeping all other feeling into a chasm of his heart. "That soft, understanding voice asking me if I was having trouble with my drinking. Oh sweet Jesus!"

I didn't have a lie prepared for this question. Before I knew what I was doing I nodded 'yes'. She touched my heart with her voice and wrapped a metaphorical arm around my shoulders by saying, 'Well, I'm a drunk myself. Come in and we will talk it over.' Jesus Christ Mike I wept like a baby. I was so relieved I just stood there sobbing and she waited until I got hold of myself."

Mike smiled in understanding but said nothing. Jack continued, "She spoke softly with little emotion as she began my education. There were no questions, so I didn't have to be alert, I could just listen. And listen I did about her disease, alcoholism, and her recovery in AA." Jack had recovered and his face took on a look of near ecstasy as he recalled the moment. "I'm sure I froze the look on my face but I tell you Mike my heart thawed as if I were standing in a spring sun. I kept blinking rapidly and blowing my nose. I was warm inside and beginning to feel the heat of the building. I was afraid to ask what was in my heart; if I could please join. I knew I didn't deserve it so I continued to attempt to sound casual as I asked 'How does one join?'"

I knew, I just knew Mike that I wasn't worthy, wouldn't meet the requirements. She disarmed me, caused a major meltdown of my emotions by saying that my simply coming there made me a member." Jack's face showed the relief he must have felt at that statement. "At this moment, Mike, I learned the true meaning of the Third Tradition; the only requirement for admission to AA is a desire to stop drinking.

The pause seemed to have stretched into a rest period so Mike spoke, "What happened this morning to bring you here?"

"I'll tell you what happened, I damn near took a drink last night, that's what happened," Jack stated matter-of-factly. "I damn near fell off the wagon and worried about it all night. My wife and I had an argument about our granddaughter marrying her black boyfriend and I got so mad I damn near did it. The only thing I could think of was to come over here and talk to you. I knew you wouldn't tell me what you would do. I knew you would listen and say nothing if there was nothing to be said and by God that is just what you did. I feel better, you got more information than you ever wanted, and I'm outta here. With that Jack stood up, grabbed Mike's hand in a firm grip then took off. The jauntiness was back in his walk. "He's going to be just fine," Mike murmured to himself. He went into the house, he wanted to view that video again.

The Wall Street journal was open but not of too much interest to him this morning. He took out the video he had retrieved from the girl's home. Running over every detail of the video of the murder he was jerked back to reality by the phone ringing. "Good morning," he said.

"You da guy looking for somebody special last night?, a raspy voice inquired.

Game on.

THE SEDUCTION

Tuscola, Illinois 1942

Upon arriving at the depot in Tuscola Michael was met by a man who introduced himself as Mr. Clark, a friend of his biological father's. He was portly and reminded Michael of one of the movie stars who had large lips and smoked a cigar. Short, heavy-set his stomach stuck out providing a bulge across which a gold watch chain draped. Taking him under his care Mr. Clark explained his father was delayed driving in from Chicago. He drove them both to the funeral parlor. Once things were arranged there he took him to lunch in a small café in town and during that time made a very peculiar observation. "Michael," he said, "I don't think you and your father are going to get along."

Michael just looked at him, not sure of how to respond to such a statement, then finally asked, "What do you mean by that sir?"

"Well son," Clark explained, rolling his cigar from one corner of his mouth to the other with his tongue, "After spending just this short time with you it is apparent that you have many traits in common, perhaps too many." Michael looked at him for a moment, noticing the food stain on his striped tie, and then looked away not understanding what he was being told. "Why," he continued, "You even have a way of brushing the crumbs off your fingers by flicking them with your thumb and your father does that too; it is startling. You have an intimidating way about you as has he and I see discord when you meet."

Michael understood but didn't care. He had to be here to bury his mother, and then he had to go home and take care of his stepfather, that's all he knew. He had begun building a wall of isolation from events long ago; probably when his biological father left. The height and breadth of this wall increased during the many times he spent in the bar waiting for his mother to get off work. She had been a waitress and played the piano in the "Pete Dupont Bar", on Grand River Avenue in Detroit. He had to learn to shut out the drunken behavior of people at a very early age; people and their actions just didn't affect him after a while. His mother, though caring, was busy making a living to see that he and his older brother had a home and schooling. He was left to his own devices early on while she worked; baby sitters and Aunts didn't exist at his house. His mother's death had added a top tier to that wall. What Clark was saying was unimportant; he had his mother to bury and then he would go home.

Michael's first stepfather, Martin, who went by the name Marty, was living with his common-law wife Colleen in Highland Park, Michigan. Marty was really not interested in having children but after divorcing his mother, did, on occasion, take him to a favorite cafeteria called Delmonico's where he delighted in the array of desserts. He also visited and stayed overnight with them at times. Marty was not interested in sports or fishing. It was at best an arms-length relationship to Marty but Michael considered him his father, called him dad and his mother had given him his last name; it wasn't until he graduated high school and had to find a birth certificate that he learned what his last name really was.

Marty had big hands and Michael had fond memories of walking with him as a small boy holding onto his little finger which was very reassuring. When he washed his red convertible he gave Michael a nickel for ever nail he found by inspecting the tires. He had a way of making him seem important at times. Marty left when he was eight years old and he remembered standing outside the red convertible crying and begging his him to stay. In later years he could still feel his heart break as he remembered his dad driving away for the last time.

This current experience at his mother's funeral was making the wall higher and wider thus shaping his outlook on life into a pragmatic disinterest. He would go through life with compassionate detachment.

His father did show up, they did meet and it was all pretty inconsequential as far as Michael was concerned. His father was short, about five feet five inches tall, slim and wore his Fedora hat like someone out of a Damon Runyon story. He had a business in Chicago and was married to a lady who had not accompanied him to Tuscola. They talked, but not at any great length, and it was obvious they had different feelings about his future since he was but sixteen years of age.

He rejected the suggestion he return to Chicago with his biological father explaining he wanted to return home to Inkster, Michigan and take care of his second stepfather Pete Trout who was recuperating. Even at the tender age of sixteen Mike was an independent soul and could make a good argument. It was agreed that he would return. They got on about the business of burying his mother.

Mike eventually returned home and he sought out Mrs. Ferrante, mother of his girlfriend Louise, for assistance in learning how to cook. Since his mother had used a small electric crock-pot she suggested a stew and after explaining the hows and wherefores assisted him in getting the ingredients. He was quite proud when his stepfather sat down to his first meal.

He watched him take a bite and anticipated the praise which he hoped would be forthcoming. What he got was a picture of a man chewing as though what he had in his mouth was rubber, with little coming back but grunts. Picking up a piece of stew meat himself he soon found that he too could not chew through it and learned later that Mrs. Ferrante had neglected to tell him to cook the meat first. When he had speared a carrot and found it tender he assumed everything was done. Pete, full of beer, was gracious enough to eat what he could and come forth with a little praise for this first effort.

Michael returned to school but fate put too many obstacles in the way of his having an ideal teen life. To compound his agony his stepfather brought home a foul-mouthed woman who drank even more than he did and the situation became unbearable. She was too drunk all the time to even consider being a mother. Michael contacted Marty and asked if he could come live with him and Colleen. It was agreed, he moved in with them and Pete was left to whatever the fates had in store for him: he never saw nor heard from him again.

Marty was a truck driver, had a slow, deliberate way of talking using his large hands extensively. He had the old southern ways about him. He loved to expound on many subjects and did so in a deep voice that soothed and invited you to listen. When asked a question or presented with an opinion diverse to his own he never challenged but sought to get his point across in a gentlemanly way. For all his southern charm he was often given to talking about "Them god dam niggers" or "Them god dam Jews." He had a Teutonic aloofness about him doling out warmth like precious diamonds, few and far between. Mike idolized him and liked it when he called him "Hambone." The day Mike crept downstairs and saw him kill the litter of puppies by crushing their heads with the handle used to shake the furnace grate was the first indication of his cool deliberate ability to do what he felt had to be done with no room for compassion; his German ancestry became apparent.

Colleen, Marty's wife, was blonde, in her late thirties and a buxom child of the old south. Her favorite subject was the tips she made as a waitress. She called Michael "Hon" and treated him royally always eager to make for him his favorite, Butterscotch pie with meringue on top. She called his stepfather "Daddy" and she would bustle about their apartment making a great to-do about cleaning and taking care of him. Colleen had plans for Michael that would further shape his personality; she intended to lure this sixteen year old boy into her bed and show him the earthly delights of sex.

It was decided that he would get a full time job and finish his schooling in night school. This was typical of Marty's frugal thinking. He had a miser's way about him and never suggested he go to a neighborhood school and live like a normal boy his age. It was simply not in Marty's nature to "mollycoddle" as he put it. Michael enrolled at the Detroit Institute of Technology for night courses. The war was in full swing so he hired in at the Gear Grind Company in Hamtramack, Michigan on the night shift with no trouble.

Marty's job of car hauling took him out of town days at a time, so Michael and Colleen were often alone. She began her seduction by explaining to him that Marty, though a wonderful man, was not home enough, not paying enough attention to her. She went so far as to confide in him that Marty was "too large" for sex and often hurt her. She began bringing the conversations more and more into the area of sex. She would ask him to dance with her and laughingly tell him how little Eddie who lived downstairs "got hard" when she danced with him. She became infatuated with him and bought him many things out of her tips.

Working from twelve midnight until eight in the morning Michael would come home and get some sleep while Colleen worked as a waitress. He would get up for dinner then go to night school which was a long bus ride to downtown Detroit. At ten o'clock he left school and took three busses to Hamtramck where he worked grinding parts for tanks. Colleen was about to begin a period of sexual intrigue that no sixteen year old boy could possibly comprehend.

As he came up the stairs at nine o'clock one morning he could hear Colleen humming happily. When he reached the top and looked into the kitchen he saw her. She was standing at the ironing board pressing something, clothed only in high heels, silk stocking with garter belt, thin silk panties and brassiere. Her thighs were milky white and full ending in the most beautiful ass cheeks, visible through the panties, he had ever seen. He couldn't speak or move as his passions fought with loyalties. He felt himself get hard as he watched her bottom jiggle when she moved, wishing he could bury his face in them. Suddenly, feigning surprise, she turned around and looked at him and said, "Oh, hi Hon, I didn't hear you." Her breasts seemed to be trying to tumble out of her bra as she wiggled her shoulders back and forth. His desire was almost too much to bear.

Apparently satisfied she had titillated him sufficiently she hurried off to her bedroom exclaiming, "I'll get a robe on Hon, sorry, I didn't hear you coming." This of course was a lie as the door opening downstairs, his heavy footsteps, all would have alerted a deaf mute. Returning to the kitchen in a filmy robe she said, "You must be hungry Hon, I'll fix you some breakfast," as she gave him the now standard hug which held his face into her cleavage. "What would you like?" Mike could see her full thighs that ended in slim ankles clearly as she stood there. This act would be performed often for him in the morning under different settings, but always with a full, nearly unadorned view, of her body in a garter belt.

Colleen apparently had decided he was ripe for the picking one Saturday morning. Arriving home at the usual time he was greeted not only with the visual but hugged with her gown left open. Once again his loyalty to his step-father and his passions collided. That evening when he was preparing to pull out the sofa bed in the front room she said, "Hon, you don't have to sleep on that lumpy old thing. Daddy won't be home for three days so you can sleep in my bed. Bring you pajamas and crawl in with me," It wasn't a request so much as it was a command. He willingly obeyed with an ambivalence of loyalty and passionate need.

The bed felt much better than the couch and Colleen's perfume was intoxicating. Filled with mixed emotions he tried to stay over to one side. She moved up behind him as he lay there, cuddling him from behind kissing his neck as she murmured goodnight. Sometime during the night he awoke to find she had slid her hand down the front of his pajamas and was fondling his penis. Mike was very large and he heard her breathing become louder as she massaged his manhood, tracing the head with her fingers, gently squeezing his testicles. He was still half asleep when she turned him towards her and gently positioned his face into her warm breasts while she continued to stroke him as she pulled his pajama bottom down and off.

Gently she pulled him up on her, guiding him into her body, and took his virginity. As soon as he entered her it felt as though she had taken him in her hand and was squeezing, letting go then squeezing again. She had developed her vaginal muscles so that she could flex them like a milking machine. Holding one of her large breasts she guided his head until his mouth opened and was full of ripe nipple and warm flesh. Her moaning and thrusting drove him on. It was the most sensuous moment in his life and he was unable to hold himself, ejaculating into her immediately as she milked him over and over. He was sixteen and virile; she was thirty and a nymphomaniac. He maintained his erection; she maintained his desire using her mouth to bring him along again and again. Nothing was said about the episode in the morning but they both knew it would happen again; she with almost morbid desire, he with mixed emotions of loyalty betrayed and passions that needed relief.

They had sex many times after that and he was never able to hold off as the pressures of her vagina made it impossible; he was milked from the moment he entered. The combination of lust and guilt was tremendous but he was helplessly in her grasp, seeking intercourse whenever he could, which was often. All the things that had happened to him created a need for the calming affect of endorphins which flowed like a refreshing stream during sex.

THE MARINE

Michael graduated high school and immediately volunteered for the Marines. World War II was under way and all able American boys wanted to fight for their country. America was under siege by Japan and England was close to succumbing to the German Army. Mexico and South America remained neutral. At 5 foot ten inches tall he was a perfect example of well-formed sinew and exactly what they were looking for. The train ride to California took two and a half days. Arriving at the station they fell out and were told to stand on yellow footprints painted on the pavement. The world according to the Corps was explained to them and they were advised that they were maggots and would now begin to be "Demaggotized."

He took his "Boot" at Camp Pendleton a former Spanish ranch of almost 125,000 acres that had been converted into a Marine training camp and named after Major General George Pendleton. In 1769 the Spaniards named it Santa Margarita since they arrived in the area on the holy day of Saint Margaret. In 1841 the Mexican governor of the Californios awarded the land to two brothers who called it Rancho Santa Margarita y Las Flores. An Englishman, John Forster, paid off the gambling debts of one of the brothers and received a deed to the land in return. His heirs had to sell the ranch to a wealthy cattleman,

James Flood. The 122,798 acre land site was bought for the Marine Corps in 1942

His first day set the tone for the rest of his tour. Having been "peeled" at the camp barbershop he stood naked at the counter in the supply Quonset hut. His new fatigues lay in front of him as the disinterested Marine PFC laid a pair of 16EE combat boots on the counter. "Hey man," he complained, making his first mistake as a Boot, "These dam things are big enough for King Kong. I wear a size nine." Just then he felt a pain in his butt. Swinging around angrily he faced a 6 foot-plus tall Marine corporal who, it turned out, was from Georgia; they were always from Georgia. This Ole Boy had a chew bulging from his jaw and he had just tried to kick his combat boot right up Mike's ass. Mike had met his first DI

"Ya'll keep yore hole shut muthafukka, drawled this antagonist. 'Ya'll shut up 'n do as yore tole or I'll kick your boot ass up the hill." The corporal's jaw muscle bulged as he ragged the new recruit. Realizing where he was Mike got his anger under control and he turned back to the counter where the man had obligingly laid out the correct size boots. He made up his mind that would never happen again and that he would obtain rank as fast as possible to assure that it wouldn't.

Ordered to be at the infirmary by 5 AM the next morning the "Boots" stood in the hallway in their green skivvies waiting to get shots. A Corpsman leaned out of a door opening with an immense hypodermic needle in this hand as he yelled, "OK, first man, let's get it done Boots." Their eyes bugged out of their heads because what he held in his hands looked like something you would use on an elephant. He obviously had gone to the motor pool and gotten a grease gun, polished it up, stuck a large piece of wire on the end and had a realistic looking "Hypodermic Needle from Hell" that had them all backing up. When they got into the room the ruse was made apparent. Mike was amused when the six foot two man in front of him wound up on the floor in a dead faint from his first shot.

In "Boot Camp" he lived in a tent with five other boots, all from different parts of the country. He learned to make his bed so that a quarter, when thrown on the top blanket, would bounce back up so he could catch it in mid-air. Scrubbing his own fatigues, sox and underwear out behind the slop chute was a daily chore. Fels Naphtha was the soap of choice and it smelled like it would eat through the fabric. The chow was plentiful and they rinsed their trays in soapy water as they left and piled them high just inside the door. They kept their knife, fork and spoon as well as their canteen cup.

Platoon Sergeant C. C. Ries, drill instructor of the 446th Platoon, wasn't a big man, about 5 feet ten inches and maybe 175 pounds but he had a thin lipped stare that told you right off that this Kentucky cracker could ruin your day; his commands hit you like a hickory stick. On their first day as "Boots" he told them that more than half of them would probably die in this war. This information prompted Mike to attempt to be the best in every form of survival technique. He became expert at hand to hand combat practicing with the K Bar fighting knife and bayonet as well as a form of Jujitsu every spare moment and whenever he could find a partner. On the last day of the last week of Boot Camp he was he was told he was going to advanced infantry training camp in the Marine Combat Training Battalion or MTB. He excelled even more than he did in Boot. One incident in particular brought him to the attention of the newly formed elite Marine Corps group known as RECON.

The day began hot and got hotter as the Santa Ana winds blew down through the pass baking the already pan-hard earth. Mike's platoon had fallen out at 4 AM, chowed down, and was well into simulated warfare by 6 AM. They had been assigned a hill to take and were being shot at, with blank ammo, by Marines on the hill simulating the enemy. There was no let up in the training with the exception of a brief respite where they opened C Rations and drank limited rations of warm water from a white Lister bag hanging in the sun. They were preparing for the real stuff on the islands where staying alive meant conservation of food and water. Finally at 3 PM they were ordered to "group up" and marched back the five miles to the tent area.

With two miles to go they came abreast of what was affectionately known as the Sand Monster. It was a hill of sand about twenty-five feet in height with a base of fifty feet. Mikes platoon was ordered up the hill, and with full pack and a day of combat simulation already under their belts, the shifting sands might as well have been pools of glue. Every step they took drove their legs into the stuff almost up to the knee; pulling them out for the next step took extreme energy, filling their combat boots with sand. All but two made it up, those two crapping out halfway with heat exhaustion.

When they got to the top the exhausted Marines had all they could do not to tumble forward as they headed down. Mike was feeling good about making it until the order came to go back up. This time two more men fell by the wayside with the only attention given being a canteen of warm water being placed in their hands. They were force-marched up and down that hill three more times losing two thirds of the platoon. Mike not only made it, he led the last charge and remained standing at the base of the hill when the others fell to the ground. Nothing on his face, except the rivulets of sweat pouring through the grime, gave any indication he couldn't do it again. Shortly thereafter Mike was summoned to Sergeant Rise's tent.

Double timing it he saw the sergeant standing outside in the hot summer sun near a clump of Mesquite with a Gunnery Sergeant who looked meaner than a junk yard dog and twice as hostile. He stopped immediately in front of Ries, came to attention yelling, "Sir, Private Granite reporting as ordered Sir!

For a moment they both just looked at him like he was the sorriest piece of humanity God had ever put on this earth.

Sergeant Ries spoke first, raising his voice to just under thunder and yelled, "This here is the meanest, baddest, worstest Marine warrior you are ever going to meet Private. He eats tires for breakfast and washes it down with battery acid. This here Gunnery Sergeant of Force Recon is without a doubt the most outstanding, most vicious and at the same time most intelligent Marine warrior on God's little green acre; he is my twin brother and you will give him your by god attention memorizing every word that comes roaring out of his mouth for they are the words of God. Are we clear Private?" he had started to turn a beet red by now.

"Sir," yelled Mike, " If the Sergeant says it then it is the word of God, Sir," with no emotion they could detect. A hint of a smile appeared on the Gunny's face, soon replaced with a dark scowl that said death was near at hand. He walked right up to him and stood so that his face was but a few inches away and yelled, "What got you into my Marine Corps sonny, were you some kinda sissy street-kid back home and they needed somebody to babysit ya? Mike stood steady with no trace of his inner feelings on his face.

"You best answer me Marine," yelled the gunny, his face even closer, eyes smoldering. "I'm the orneriest tiger you are ever gonna come across and I don't cotton to those what don't answer my questions."

"I got in to fight the Japanese Gunny because they want me to kiss their Jap asses and I don't kiss anybody's ass, Sir," Mike yelled back.

"I am the avenging God of Force Recon, Marine," Gunny yelled, "and that means I control hell itself. A Recon Maine has no equal. A Recon Marine is feared by the enemy and if you kill him you just make him mad. "I want killers Private, I want mean sons-a-bitches and violent men that I can mold into fighting machines with the bravery of a Sioux warrior combined with the intelligence of a scientist topped of with the compassion of a hungry lion.

Does that describe you private?" he asked dropping the volume about twenty decibels so it was only ear shattering.

"Sir, yes Sir," Mike responded standing even taller now wanting in every way possible to be part of this Marine's Force Recon.

His efforts were rewarded with Private First Class Stripes and he was sent to Radio Intelligence School on Bremerton Island just off Seattle to learn Japanese code. The school was a tough taskmaster keeping them in class ten hours a day, six days a week listening to and copying Japanese radio stations.. Liberty was used to travel to Seattle via a ferryboat that made the journey in 45 minutes. Anyone that talked about what they did at the school was never seen again. When he came in from shore leave on Sunday evening he would hear his sleeping mates ditting and dahing in their sleep having been so immersed in the technique of code copying they were practicing in their dreams.

Upon completing school he found it was to prepare him for the newly organized 2nd Marine Raider Battalion formed quietly and specifically for a raid on Makin Atoll in the British-mandated Gilbert Islands. They were the brain child of Lieutenant Colonel Carlson and known as Carlson's Raiders." Carlson, lean and flint hard, had gone to China, observed the guerrilla action against the Japanese and brought the techniques back to form two Raider groups. The "Exec" was Major James Roosevelt, son of President Roosevelt. They were an elite group that excelled in hand-to-hand combat and living off the land with emphasis on survival training under unimaginable hardships. They were the original "Search and Destroy" warriors; America's best to do America's worst.

GHOST WARRIORS

At the beginning of World War II Makin Island was made a target because if the Japanese were allowed to continue to supply it the communication line with Australia would be disrupted and Samoa would be taken shortly thereafter. The mission was for the newly formed Marine Raiders to land by submarine before dawn, destroy all communications, kill every Japanese soldier on the island then evacuate by nightfall. They did land with much trouble from the reef, accomplished their mission and were taken off at dusk leaving nine live marines behind, as they did not arrive at "Zero Hour". It was determined later these nine were taken to Kwajalein and beheaded.

After the successful campaign on Makin the Raiders defeated the Japanese on Tulagi, invaded Guadalcanal on August 7 of '42 and Bougainville in November of '43. The Japanese began to refer to them as the "Ghost Warriors." In February of 1944 the technique of "Leapfrogging", bypassing islands with large concentrations of Japanese soldiers, had saved thousands of lives. It took the Marines North to the Marshall Islands where they took and secured Kwajalein and Enewetak. They leapfrogged Truk, bombing it instead to make it unusable as an air base thus stranding the large Japanese contingent stationed there. In August they had occupied Guam, Saipan and Tinian working through the end of 1944.

The 4th Marines known as the OBCM (Old Breed China Marines) reformed around the Raider battalions commanded by Colonel Alan Shapley, one of Annapolis's great athletes.

With the Raiders they were combined into the 6th Division to fight the last great battle of the Pacific Theatre, Okinawa code-named ICEBERG!

The U.S. had planned to invade Formosa prior to invading Japan itself. In 1944 Admiral Chester W. Nimitz, Commander in Chief of the Pacific Fleet (CINCPAC), argued against such action. He felt General Douglas Mac Arthur should take Luzon and the Philippines while he directed action against Iwo Jima and Okinawa. It would use more than half a million men and over 1,500 ships.

General Simon Bolivar Buckner, a Kentuckian, was selected to run the expeditionary force for the amphibious phase of Project Iceberg. A big man that liked to take risks and grind ahead with maximum firepower he had an instinct for tactics. He came from a background of soldiering; his grandfather had been a Confederate General. Intelligence had come down from General Eisenhower's camp that the Nips had Jet aircraft now copied from their German allies. Ike wanted to get hold of one and had a report that such a plane had crashed somewhere on Okinawa. Further word was the Nips didn't know where it had crashed so if the Americans could get to it first it could mean a lot to the American air force. He had ordered his Exec Colonel Shapner to look into it. The Colonel assured him he would get right on it.

"See that you do Colonel," snapped the General, We know the Japs got Intel from Hitler's boys about jet engines and their naval air force now has what they call the Fire Dragon. Now we have a Jap Zero, that's a navy plane and we have an Oscar, that's an army plane but we need a Dragon to look at. Word is they lost one over Guam and we need someone to go in there and find it. Once we do we can find a way to get it out. We want to do this before we attack the island if we can".

"Shap" as he was known could have been a poster Maine. 'Lean, mean and never serene' they said about him. A Kentuckian he could shoot the eye out of a squirrel at 200 yards before he was 12 years old. His most often used expression was "Hold the God Dam Phone." "Well shit," exclaimed Shapner looking at his Exec. Captain Billy Roy Martin known as "Bama". "Just how in the hell am I supposed to come up with somebody to insert into an island we're going to attack to find something that may not exist?"

Bama, came from Guntersville, Alabama, heart of TVA territory. He was big, to the point of being lumbering, and had an easy way about him and he loved to tell how a German, Gunter, married the daughter of a Cherokee chief to get the land now named after him. He once grabbed a BAR in each hand and charged a Nip machine gun post to clean it out single-handedly; the Browning Automatic Rifle was heavy enough for one man, brandishing two of them was quite a feat. "I know of a Gyrene that would fit the bill Colonel," drawled Bama. "I did boot camp with him. Kept in touch and the latest I heard he was with the new Raider Battalion. 'Name's Mike Granite. "Well sir on maneuver's one day Mike was explaining to me that reconnoitering should be done by putting a man on the ground using a parachute before an invasion. That way he could radio information to commanders about ground troops, their placement and strength."

"That would be one hell of an insertion," quipped the Colonel. "Besides, any plane going over for a drop would be shot out of the air or worst case would show them were he landed. He would be on the butcher's block in minutes. Those Japs love to decapitate. I know how many children they practiced on in China."

"Well sir this Mike has a plan and I think we ought to get him here and see what it is." The Colonel was impressed with the sincerity of this man who had save his life once and made a quick decision. "See that it's done," he shot back over his shoulder and left.

Mike Granite's competency in hand-to-hand combat was highlighted on his record; his exploits had earned him a battlefield commission of Lieutenant. His unique ability to work alone set him apart. He had taught himself Japanese and was versed in the Bushido Code.

Arriving on New Guinea he was sped into the hidden area of Intel Quarters where he was asked to wait. It wasn't long before he was escorted in the office area of Colonel Shapner. He snapped off a sharp salute, "Granite reporting for duty *Sir.*"

"At ease Granite were gonna keep this short and sweet. Bamma here is trying to convince me you have an idea that will help us get the Intel about Okinawa that we need. Lay it out for me."

"Well Sir". Mike began," I happen to know that TAI has a secret plane they constructed from German plans that can fly faster and higher than anything we have ever had. Tactical Airborne Intelligence is a super secret group that continually researched what the enemy has in fixed wing aircraft.

"Go on." said the Colonel settling back in his chair and putting his feet up on the desk.

"Well sir the Germans have an Austrian genius with an idea of an aircraft that was all wing. It was called the New York Bomber because they intended to drop a highly destructive bomb of some sort on New York which would detonate above ground spreading some sort of nuclear waste, then return to Germany."

"Go on," responded the Colonel, thoroughly involved now.

"My G2 tells me we have a unit under wraps that can hit over 45,000 feet. I have quite a bit of experience in electronic transducers," Mike continued, "and I could rig a barometric unit to act as a switch. If they got me high enough and released me in a sphere, like a ball, …

"Hold the goddam phone there marine, what do you mean by a sphere?"

"A ball Sir, made out of the new plastic our guys have been talking about. I could fit into a plastic ball in the fetal position with a oxygen bottle and be dropped from 30,000 to 40,000 feet. There would be room for just me a parachute some weaponry and a radio or course. The barometric transducer could be set to open at a minimal distance from the ground and I could black-chute in. Once on the ground I could take a look-around and transmit the info back to a sub.

The Colonel was in for a dollar now. He turned to his aide and said, "Get a coded message out to the "spooks" with this idea and let's see if the ground trembles. Do it now!"

Traveling on VOCG (Verbal Order of the Commanding General) Mike arrived at a secret airport. The Modified TR-1 aircraft stood like a needle in the darkness, sprays of moonlight careening of its body. It was the latest from the secret archives of the intelligence community able to fly at extreme altitudes. It was the precursor of the U2, which would be shot down 20 years later over Russia in May of 1960. Carrying cameras made by Chicago Aerial Industries in Barrington, Illinois it could register an automobile in detail at 40,000 feet. The underside had been rigged with a parachute-type release and to that was the sphere Mike was to travel in to be dropped over Guam. .

His face painted in camouflage colors, his jaw set in determination Mike stood looking at his "Jungle Chariot" as he called it. It was a beast all right he thought to himself, an impressive beast and he was going to ride it. Only three other men were present including the pilot, as this was a clandestine mission with only a selected few at the top aware of its mission. As it turned out, it never happened; not in this chariot anyway. As he was preparing to enter the plane a jeep came jolting up carrying a PFC with orders to stand down.

THE BOG

The voice on the other end of the line was course like gravel and Mike responded with care to the question as to whether or not he was the guy asking questions.

"That's correct," he responded, "Who is this?"

"Let me ax ya sumthin," was the response, "How bad ya wanna know?"

"It depends on the information. If you give me a location I will give you $100.00. If it checks out I'll give you $100.00 more," said Mike.

"Five hundred clams and no other deal. Take it or leave it," the voice said with finality.

"I'll take it," said Mike. Where can I meet you?"

"Deres a place near Richmond on route 31 called Glacial Park....

"I know the place," Mike interrupted.

"Let me finish," said the caller with irritation. "Go into da park past da barn on da right and drive to da parking lot by da gate. Park 'n walk nort past the marsh up to the bog. I'll meet ya by da bog. And come alone. I'll be able to watch ya all da way. Tomorrow morning at 8 o'clock and bring cash, nuttin else. O.K.?

"I'll be there," said Mike hanging up. He felt foreboding but refused to spend any time with it. If violence were to come he would approach swiftly, head on and deal with it as he remembered something he once heard. "Heroes die once, a coward dies many times.

The next morning he left the house at 7 AM taking Northwest Highway east through Crystal Lake to Route 31. The sky immediately above was clear with an occasional wisp of cloud but a sheet of gray hung over the area up ahead like a stadium dome. Turning north on route 31 he headed into McHenry where it jogged east then north again. Up ahead he spotted the sign identifying the entrance to Glacial Park. He turned left and headed down the long stretch of road towards the entrance. The field on the left was black due to a controlled-burn making the day seem even more ominous.

Glacial Park covered 2,806 acres just outside of Richmond and is called the "crown jewel" of Mc Henry County Conservation District. Often filled with hikers and campers it offered guided tours and cross county skiing in the winter along its 6.7 miles of interconnected trails and camping sites. It has a number of Kames and in addition, many special programs and educational workshops are held at various times throughout the year in the park's nature center. The bog the caller had referred to was the Leather Leaf bog filled with poison Sumac and wild cranberry. The barn he referred to was used for educational purposes and always had some sort of display going on for the public.

Passing the barn on the right and following the road he came to the parking area by a locked swing-gate. He pulled in, got out of the car, removed his "dittybag" from the rear that held all his "essentials" as he liked to call them and proceeded to cross the road. A sign called attention to the marsh on the right from which a cacophony of frog sounds emanated to the delight of many ducks and geese residing thereon. A genderless stick figure invited him to walk the path that was strewn with bark chips and led north to a small wooded area.

He became very cautious as he approached the area noticing a resting bench just up a small incline and under the canopy of trees into which he emerged after climbing the hill. The only sound was the buzz of a plane passing overhead. Beyond on the left was a sign identifying the Coyote Trail and before him lay the Leather Leaf Bog, the prearranged point of contact with an arrow pointing to a walkway of pontoons that provided a path skirting the bog for viewing. Stepping onto the pontoons he felt them give under his weight and he looked out upon a sea of bronze foliage of Poison Sumac. It was quiet and just a bit threatening. He mused over the memories he had from his childhood of the "Boogey Man" a legend that came from men, who lived on bogs, rushing out at people frightening them almost to death; they were originally called "Boggy Man."

He remained motionless feeling that something was wrong here. Where in the hell was his contact? He jerked his head to look in the direction of a muffled sound; it was a deer poking about in the trees. As his eyes followed the animal they picked out an abnormal form for this environment lying along the rim of the bog. Walking cautiously he came upon the body of a man. "Shit," he muttered, "This dude won't be talking."

Here was the man he was supposed to get information from as to the whereabouts of one of the men who killed his friend's daughter and her children. Mike looked around for blood and found none. He turned the body over and drew back quickly as he stared in to a grotesquely contorted face indicating the victim had died while in a great deal of pain. Taking out his laptop computer he extended the antennae from the side, turned it on and locked onto the G87 geosynchronous satellite the CIA allowed him to use. His work with them and the FBI immediately after the war had earned him many useful friends. Utilizing a USB connection he plugged in his virtual retinal display glasses. The VRD's were manufactured by Microvision in Seattle and had a tiny screen abut two inches from his eye on which was displayed a video screen. He put a Blue Tooth receiver button in his ear. Dialing the phone number of the FBI database he waited for the handshake signal that told him he was locked on. When it came he turned to the victim.

He carefully placed the deceased's finger on his Biometrics Scanner waiting for the unit to recognize the print. The 200-hertz tone told him there was no recognition. Using a USB port Mike attached his video camera taking shots of the face focusing on the area around the eyes and ear shape and size. He ran it over the right hand looking for a three dimensional clarification as well as the pattern of veins on the back and ridges and valleys on the palm.

There was no response. Carefully he opened the eyelid focusing the companion laser onto the iris area. Again the non-recognition tone came through. "Dam," he muttered, "wouldn't you know I would get a goat. What the hell good is biometrics if they won't give you data?"

Dropping the line he found an up-link to another satellite and dialed the Museum of Science and Industry. When the operator answered he asked for Dr. William Fish. He and Bill had spent time together on Okinawa after they mopped it up. Bill was a forensic anthropologist and was there to help identify corpses. "Hello," he heard him answer recognizing the Midwestern twang. "Bill, its Mike Granite and I need your help right away".

Well I'll be damned", responded Bill, "Where the hell are you anyway?"

"I'm up north and I have a corpse I need help with. I want to show it to you and have you work some of your magic" he answered.

"Show me a corpse? How you go'nna to that?" queried Bill.

"I've linked onto a satellite using WAP," he answered. That's Wireless Application Protocol and it allows me to use my mini-cam and send you video. Do you have DSL because I need high speed and as much bandwidth as possible.

"I got the high speed connection. What am I going to look at?"

"I've got a body, a goat, and I need help right away identifying cause and time of death as closely as possible.

"You called me here for a dam goat?"" exclaimed Bill. "What you need is a vet!"

"Not an animal dam it," said Mike mildly irritated, "A goat is a person who is an unstable biometrics data source. It may come from the Greek word for tragedy, which is *tragos, which* means *goat.* As you know biometrics is the science of measuring unique physical characteristics of an individual for identification. Swirls on the fingertip, blood vessel pattern, the micro-visual pattern of the retina, geometry of appendage, facial appearance and of course voice patterns can all be used for ID."

"I've heard a little about that," interrupted Bill, "how does it apply to me?"

Let me finish," continued Mike. "Goats often cause false rejections. We don't know why but the only way to work with them is by Layered Biometric Authentication process or LBA.

We take two or more characteristics to ID them. I have run the fingerprints to no avail and obviously can't use anything else because he's dead. This is where you come in."

"Gotcha", responded Bill enthusiastically, "You want a little forensic anthropology. Keep in mind that we can get a lot on insect activity around a corpse. Any temperature below 40 degrees keeps that to a minimum and presents a problem." Mike asked him to explain about insects.

"Well", Bill began, "Word is it started in China around 1200BC. There was a murder and the assassin had used a rice sickle on the victim. The head of the village called everyone together and had him or her lay his or her sickle in front of him. When flies landed on just one of the tools the man confessed. For a long time forensic people considered maggots as nothing more than revolting but we can now we use them to fix the date and time of death fairly accurately. By the way, entomologists can also be called in to determine where a shipment of Marijuana came from by the insects he finds."

"Where do they get bodies to run data on?" inquired Mike.

"Many people donate their bodies to science," Bill explained, "Also the bodies of derelicts that nobody claims are available. The University of Tennessee has a "body farm" called the "Human Decay Research facility" or HDRF. Here they have human corpses laying outside in various degrees of decay. Some are in trunks of old cars and they may place one over a log to simulate a hunting accident to study what insects arrive each day. They also collect and inspect larvae in the lab and knowing the gestation period of the critters come pretty close to the time of death. Insects come to a body in waves or faunal succession. First flies such as blow, flesh and houseflies come to feast and lay eggs. Ants show up with dung flies and beetles close behind. The aroma of rotting flesh in various stages of decay calls each one. They also look to see what birds are nearby to feed on the insects.

"Interesting," commented Mike, "Can I transmit video now?

"Stand by one", Bill interrupted. After a few seconds he was back on the line. "You may fire when ready Gridley," he joked. Mike began his transmission.

"Excellent, excellent," Bill chortled. "Coming through five by five," taking them both back to the late 1940's. "I see the body is on its stomach. Lift the shirt so I can see his back. That's it. Well I can tell you this. This guy wasn't killed here as indicated by the discoloration of the back. The blood settles to the down side so it means he lay top down for a while then was deposited here. Point the camera at the nostrils and get up close. Nope, no maggots or even the sign of a fly. They can smell death a mile away as the odor floats in tiny packets of molecules on the wind in bunches that tend to stay clumped. They go for the moist areas first. Pull the camera back so I can see the head. Uh huh! There's nothing around the eyes or ears either. The eggs look like finely grated cheese laid out in a line. This person wasn't killed here and hasn't been here very long.

"I was afraid of that," said Mike. "Someone wanted me to figure out this is a warning for me to lay off."

Show me his hands," asked Bill. Mike zoomed in on the left palm adjusting for focus. He heard Bill muttering to himself. "Well," he mused, "your man has something to do with the ocean or fish market. The leathery, wrinkled condition of the skin shows that. It's the kind of thing that brine or salt solution would precipitate. Now go on up to the head area and let me see his face." Mike adjusted the camera hurriedly as he was becoming concerned about the police showing up. There was a long pause then Bill exclaimed, "I'll be damned, it doesn't make sense but it does seem to corroborate the skin condition. The grimace on the face and the coloration I have seen on corpses that died from the sting of Sea Wasps."

"What in the name of hell is a Sea Wasp?" Mike asked.

"It's a form of jellyfish that injects a poison deadlier than snake venom. It kills in less than three minutes and the pain is such the face contorts much like your victim there. Yep, a lot like a sea wasp sting," Bill remarked again.

"I can't figure that," responded Mike incredulously. His eye had caught a slight flash on his left and his head and body changed position instinctively. The bark of a tree directly in line with where his head had been exploded outward and he fell to the ground turning his head in what he had instantly had perceived to be the line of fire.

"What was that?" yelled Bill.

"I'm under fire. The SOB must have a sniper's rifle, stand by one." He remained in a prone position behind the trunk and opened his "ditty bag" which he wore like a backpack and took out a mirror with a telescoping handle. He adjusted it so he could see over the Poison Sumac to the other side of the bog. Seeing nothing he took out another package and began assembling a small airplane. "Mike!" He heard Bill's concerned call, "You O.K.?"

"Yea, I'm fine. I'm setting up my MAV. I want to see just what the hell is stalking me."

"You've got more dam toys. Now what's an MAV?"

He kept working as he replied. "It's a micro air vehicle made by Aerovironment. They've got the technique down so well it's punched out of a sheet of silicon. This one is called the Gnat it's so small. It is 4 inches long, weighs under a pound and uses an RCM for propulsion as well as MEMS for navigation coordinates." He had hot-wired the device to his computer, which had a fire wire connector.

Are you going to explain RCM and MEM'S?" inquired Bill now demanding details.

A picture showed up on the computer screen indicating satellites available. He clicked on one and waited for the lock-on tone, which came immediately. He typed in the compass direction and his estimate of the distance to target then waited for the system to program the coordinates into the MEMS system of the aircraft. "MEMS," he answered, "are Micro Electro Mechanical Systems and are used somewhat like an accelerometer. RCM means Reciprocating Chemical Muscle Propagation system. I'm using a syringe to inject fuel into the RCM, which will cause a chemical reaction that generates a gas causing the wings to flap. It's that simple." He finished as he released the craft, watching it climb then head for the target area.

A picture of the changing landscape was on the computer screen. "It carries a micro-miniature video camera weighing less than a quarter of an ounce" he continued, "the predecessor of the one used to view the human alimentary canal when swallowed. The MIT Lincoln Lab, using charge-coupled diodes for a definition of one hundred thousand by one hundred thousand pixels, developed for the military. Stand by one," he said curtly as the area he wanted came into view. There, crouching next to a tree with his rifle resting on a branch was his would-be assassin. "Gotcha," he said.

"Got who?" Queried Bill, "who have you got on your wonder widget and what in hell…

"Listen Bill," he interrupted, "I'm signing off. I want to nail this bastard. I'm gonna leave the beacon on and I'll be in touch.

"Wait a minute," protested Bill, "tell me where you are so I can send somebody…"

Mike cut him off and proceeded to gather up his equipment. Throwing three small plastic encapsulated packages different distances from where he stood he slithered along like he did as a sniper in the war. He reached a dense patch of trees where he could crouch and using a compass proceeded in a semicircle being careful not to cause any foliage to wave a greeting to his would-be assassin. He was hoping not to disturb any birds, which would fly up giving away his position. Arriving at a point he calculated would put him perpendicular to the sniper he took a small transmitter from his pocket, activated the switch and pressed. Immediately a sharp report came from one of the packets he had dropped previously.. He watched as the sniper fired in that direction. The flame from the barrel was prominent so he was able to calculated back from its tip about the length of what a rifle would be and there he saw the assailant hidden in the leaves. Long hair topped by a slouch hat prevented him from seeing the face entirely so he kept moving in that direction locking his eyes on the man's head until he felt he was close enough. Staring straight ahead he removed a Shuriken from his belt selecting it by thumb pressure which indicated it was a non-lethal variety.

Close enough now he rose up taking careful aim and hurled the Shuriken in an underhanded manner. It whistled through the air landing in the man's upper back with a muffled thud. He rose up clawing at his back then fell to the ground immobilized by the fluid that spurted out of the weapon on contact.. "Got'cha" muttered Mike moving up quickly.

He stood looking at the man on the ground. In combat the first thing he would have looked for in this situation would have been a backup; not doing so cost him.

He detected the soft plop of a silenced weapon and had started to drop to the ground instinctively, but not soon enough. Blood spurted out of his head spattering the wood chips that few from the tree when the bullet hit, pitching him forward over the prostate body of his victim. The instantaneous spurt of terror was replaced immediately by quiet, only a loon could be heard now. The swish, swish sound of someone walking through tall grass became louder and soon a figure dressed in cammos came up and rolled him off his victim. He tried to revive his cohort and unable to do so he grabbed him by the collar and dragged him through the brush in the direction he came from to their SUV leaving Mike for dead. He hurried as he had heard in the distance the mobile radio which meant a park ranger had shown up and may have heard the shot. He was gone as quickly as he had appeared.

Ten minutes later a park ranger stood over Mike's prostate body calling in his find over a 2-way. "Squawk" Looks like we got a homicide on our hands" he spoke into the radio.

THE SIGHTING

Ginger traced the scar on his temple with her finger as they lay in the afterglow of their lovemaking enjoying the melodic strains of "The Swan" from "Carnival of the Animals." Stretching occasionally like satisfied felines and rising meant losing that. "It's amazing to think that but for an eighth of an inch you would be dead now", she mused. Mike still had a small bump on his head where it had contacted a tree when his head snapped back. The blow had knocked him out and probably saved his life along with the quick action of the park ranger. He didn't know it but this day would put that incident to shame.

"Some coffee and breakfast would make it a perfect morning," he said. He watched her as she rose and walked to get her robe. The sight of her full, round cheeks through her filmy negligee always set him off. In her robe, as she left the room, she coquettishly bent over slightly raising the gown exposing even further the warm haven of love he knew so well. "You've been mooned, see you below" she said and was gone.

"Well it is time," Mike groaned, relishing the deep feeling he held for this woman. Like Rita she was Catholic and unlike her, angry at the archdiocese. Her ex had been given an annulment after 35 years and four children. Her Polish ancestry showed up in her blonde hair and full figure topped off what she said her sisters called jugs, full, meaty thighs and an almost insatiable appetite for sex. She was a registered nurse and had recently gone into home health. She had just turned 50 and told him that this age was when women really came into their own insofar as sexual freedom was concerned.

They had met at the Sundance Saloon, a place jammed on Saturday night with those who enjoyed Country Western Dancing. He had asked her to dance the "Cotton Eyed Joe" during which she told him she had been watching him and hoped he would ask her. He liked her frankness and they remained together all evening drinking wine and dancing every dance. She invited him to come home with her explaining it was the first time she had ever done so the first time meeting a man.

Her apartment was friendly, not over-decorated with a blue motif. They sat on the couch talking, both realizing they had had enough to drink. He decided to be forthright and brought up the subject of love-making to which she was appropriately shy but agreed providing he had protection. He explained he didn't and once again faced her hesitation which also melted away. He stayed the night and when they awoke Mike opened her pajama top and began nibbling as he pulled her leg up over his hip. He stoked her pubic hairs knowing they would send a message to her nervous system to enhance her pleasure. Gently he massaged her moist opening with the tip of his finger feeling her pull him into her breast with deep sighs totally into the extreme pleasure he was imparting. He began increasing the speed until he heard her utter a stuttering sound as she clamped her legs together in orgasm. Mounting her his trusts were deep and brought about another, inter-vaginal orgasm that left her trembling as he gave all he had in his own release. They lay together, him propped on his elbows so as not to put all his weight upon her, not wanting to end it.

The morning sun bathed the kitchen with a warm glow, sliding in the kitchen window that faced south, fanning out over the light green wallpaper and yellow walls. The percolator was filling the room with that welcoming aroma of morning coffee.. She had mastered the technique of getting the smell one used to get when entering restaurants that served the best. "How about eggs and sausage with sourdough toast?" she asked.

""Fine" said Mike coming up behind her with an embrace that ended with his hands cupping her breasts.

"Careful," she quipped, "I may not be done with you. His hands smoothed her gown and ended up caressing the "v" between her thighs.

"Perhaps breakfast at the "Y"," he kidded

"You've had that and more," she replied, "Talk like that and you will get a good tongue-lashing." She bent over and kissed him passionately as he squeezed her breast gently, twirling her nipple between his finger tips. "You have got to stop. The morning is going fast. Besides," she said pulling away, "We have somewhere to go this morning."

I know, I know," he groused, "You want me to go to diddle your fairy."

"It's Fair Diddley and I like to see the handiwork of all the craft people. And it is for a good cause; the mental health group puts in on. The square will be a busy place today. So let's get on with it. I told you last night I've got this dam charting to do and it takes forever," her face took on the scowl that always accompanied any discussion of *charting*.

"Why in hell you left hospital work for home health care I'll never know," Mike said. "From what you've told me you work too long and put on too many miles.

"Because, my love, when I was a hospital nurse I often had to work triple shifts and participate in things I felt were morally wrong."

"Such as?" Mike asked as he sat at the table to enjoy his coffee.

"Such as using advanced life support on patients trying to die because it was time. We used methods on seniors that should only be used in trauma and injury situations, not for the frail elderly on a downward spiral from multi-system failure. Many of these are people whose brain functions will never return to normal. The *life at any price* just doesn't make sense and angered me. Life is a fatal disease and death should be given its due when the time is right."

"Don't some doctors over treat because of possible lawsuits from relatives?" asked Mike.

"Of course," she responded with an exasperated sigh, "Of course they do. But I am concerned about the emphasis on life-prolonging technology that may add years to a devastatingly poor quality of life. The consequences both psychologically and financially can be cataclysmic. Death is not an adversary; it is a normal part of life. I wanted to focus on the quality of life issues and they wouldn't have it."

She sat across from him, shoulders drooping with the burden of it all. "Let me give you an example. When we code a patient they can become what we call *'practice meat'* for doctors in training. It is considered an opportunity for all to sharpen their skills. I know the patient is, to all intents and purposes dead, but do their families know that over-treating their loved ones becomes almost a sport for some unfeeling types?" She had retreated into a shell of depression.

Mike rose, went around the table to kneel next to her, putting his arm around her shoulder while he kissed the top of her head. "Of course you do my love. You spend all your working hours ministering to people who are deathly ill and dying and who are closer to the end than to the beginning of life. Your world would depress Jesus Christ. All you see and hear is desperation. You should try to look at it as your way of easing others who need help. What you do is a marvelous thing but when you leave each house you have to leave the patient also."

"That is good advice, darling," she replied, "But as soon as I take out a chart it reminds me of the patient." She stood up. "Let's get the hell out of here before I commit suicide."

It was warm this 21st day of May. The streets in and around the park were laid with bricks befitting a time many years ago; it added to the charm of the square and its bandstand. A breeze accompanied the activities past rows of white tents carrying the crafts of people from all over, some from as far away as Texas. It was a gentle eddy of bodies some moving clockwise and some in the opposite direction. It seemed rather like a swarm of lethargic bees moving around a hive. The fair organizers had missed the chance to be colorful with the tents and there was no music. Women haggled over clothing as their men stood idly by. Many were heard to say 'I can make it cheaper than that' and then move on to the next assassination. The heavy odor of cooking Brats wafted over the area. Four dollars got you a plate of beans and chips with a Brat on a Bun. Not much of an attempt was made to get rid of the flies and bees that circled around the condiment table with its mustard, ketchup and sweet relish. Woe be it to the person who didn't keep the top of his beverage can covered and swallowed a bee on an expedition for sugar.

One of the busiest places was the tent processing fresh popcorn called Kettle Corn. Mike watched as the owner put oil into a large cauldron adding salt and sugar then the kernels.

The line of people waiting was quite long. Some chatted with a friend while the popcorn chatted with the kettle; others started counting when their children acted up "All right Robbie I said stop it ONE, TWO, THREE", still other just shuffled by silently. As quick as he made a batch it was gone in long, clear plastic bags.

On a hot day the blast furnace fire under the kettle must make the tent extremely uncomfortable; somewhat like the tents on Guam in 1944, he thought.

A carriage offering free rides picked its way through the crowds, turned to go past the local movie house then around the periphery of the square. The horse looked perpetually tired making his way lethargically like he wished it were over. Horses being what they are there was a box tied so it hung just below and under the tail. Any excrement was caught and disposed of later. Mike swung Ginger around so she could see the animal as it started to relieve itself. "Now that my dear is what used to cover city streets by the ton. On a hot summers day the odor was overwhelming until they got it cleaned up. Then of course there was the problem of what the hell to do with it. Oh yes, those were the good old days." Ginger sniffed and turned away, proceeding with her walk, pulling him by the hand.

They stopped in front of the "Sno Cone" booth and watched the procedure. It appeared they had too many people inside the booth area as they bumped into each other constantly. There seemed to be much ado about the washing of hands; what appeared to be an inspector stood by writing on a clip board. A young man scooped ice cubes into a grinder. He reached around to throw a switch, which turned on a motor. It sounded like a chipper used by the park service when they turn branches into mulch. As shaved ice poured out a young girl scooped it into cone cups, compressed it then handed it to a lady next to her who then squirted various colored fluids onto the ice; Mike counted four squirts. It was handed to the customer who then handed the attendant a dollar. Ginger turned again to leave pulling him with her.

She began to look at jewelry while he looked into the park at the gazebo and civil war statue put there by the Ladies Auxiliary. With so many tents lining the narrow brick walks in the park some had to walk on the grass to let others pass. It was congested and as his gaze strayed to the center, he froze. There, just past the statue, was the face he had burned into his memory. The gaunt features belonged to the man he was searching for; the Jerry Colona mustache and the scar on the right temple.

This was one of the faces he saw on the video from the dead woman's home. He forgot Ginger entirely as he pushed his way through the throng striving to reach his target. Not wanting to be discourteous he often stepped aside for a lady pushing a stroller trying desperately to keep his quarry in sight. He lost him then picked him up further away heading out of the park area. He became a predator and his prey was just ahead. The man turned to look in his direction as Mike reached the statue his gaze locked on his quarry. An instinct told him Mike was a pursuer. He pulled out a 38 police special. Pandemonium broke out when someone yelled, "*GUN!*" Mike dropped to the ground as a piece of the statue exploded next to him. The ricochet hit a young woman in the throat causing blood to spurt all over her chest and some of the crowd.

Panic set in. People didn't know whether to fall to the ground or run so most of them ran. Mike raised his head and saw the man running towards the Opera House. Just then one of the auxiliary policemen came around the south opening of the park, gun drawn, yelling for the guy to put down the weapon. That was a mistake as evidenced by part of his head flying upward exposing his brain to the elements. He crashed against the bricks as Mike rose to continue the pursuit. A second shot crossed the park exploding the window of "Everest Furnishings" showering glass on the people lying on the sidewalk.

As Mike turned to look to his right the gunman stepped out from behind a food cart leveling his gun right at his head. He couldn't miss. Just then the horse pulling the carriage reared up. A young man trying to leave the area on his bike had run into its rump and skidded across the rough surface of the bricks his arms and back leaving a skid mark of blood. His body hit the shooter's leg just before discharge sending the bullet skyward. Adding to the pandemonium were the shrieking sirens of police cars. Cops boiled out of them brandishing weapons looking in every direction trying to find the source of the problem. The warm spring day once subdued and Thomas Kincaidesque was now a scene of panic. His shot ruined, the man took off again in the direction of "Cobblestones Fine Goods."

In front of Cobblestones he turned left going down a set of concrete steps to a lower level. Once there he pulled out a cloth cap putting it on to change his appearance. He also took off his light jacket and turned it inside out so that the orange showed. He did so at a measured pace being careful not to walk too quickly and draw attention. As Mike came around the same corner he saw his target go into the ""Junction" coffee emporium at the train depot. There was a train ready to leave for Chicago and he could go out the other door and board it. Running fast Mike drew the attention of a police car that pulled in front of him expelling officers with drawn guns. "On the ground Mac," one of them ordered, "On the ground. Do it now Mac, right now," he continued. Mike realized they weren't going to listen to him so he prostrated himself and they cuffed him. They made him lay on the ground ignoring what he was trying to tell them. He heard the train pull out of the station as he lay there handcuffed.

After intense interrogation the police let him go. He headed back to the park at a jog worried about Ginger. He found her sitting up against the brick wall of the gazebo safe and sound. "What in gods name was that all about?" She asked nervously. "The first thing I know you take off like a shot and all hell breaks out." She was angry, confused and wanted answers.

"I saw some nut with a gun," Mike lied not wanting to involve her yet. "I spotted him and tried to take him down but he got away. Just as well I suppose."

"Mike, I don't believe you," she countered, "I don't for a minute think you would put yourself in harms way on a whim. Now what the hell is going on here?" He told her the whole story.

"Jesus Christ Mike, are you out of your mind? Call the goddam police don't revert to Marine Corps policy of charging into the goddam guns." She wiped a worry tear from her eye then came over and hugged him tightly. "You scared the hell out of me. I can't handle theatrics like that. Promise me you won't do things like that again. Now promise me goddam it and mean it." Later he fixed a cup of coffee and sat on the back deck going over the preceding activities; Ginger had gone home. A plane flew overhead and looking up he said quietly, "Well I'll damned if it doesn't look like the old R5C1 I flew in to Enewetok.

ENEWETOK - THE INSERTION

Naval Intelligence had decided to "shit can" Mike's idea of being dropped from a futuristic aircraft and instead has assigned an "old reliable" to the job, an R5C1.

Basically a series of small islands surrounding a lagoon, Enewetok was taken by the Marines in February of 1944 and wasn't much more that a layover point. Mike stood looking at the selected aircraft, a Commando R5C1 put out by Curtiss-Wright Corporation. Starting out as a commercial airliner it made a name for itself with the Army and Marine Corps giving tremendous support during the Iwo Jima campaign, making 79 flights to evacuate wounded. One of Hollywood's luminaries, Tyrone Power, flew one of them. The paint job, gray on top and blue on the bottom was to make it difficult to see from the above or below and gave it the appearance of an Orca Killer whale. It could carry up to 36 passengers with two 2,000 horsepower Pratt and Whitney engines at a speed of up to 270 MPH at 15,000 feet. He would jump from this in daylight and take his chances.

The plane took off at 0400 hours, growled down the runway, lifted up heavily and began heading for the island of Guam in the Marianna's currently under siege by the Marine

Corps and Army. Mike sat strapped into one of the bucket seats feeling every bump and jar as it took to the air to settle into a constant vibration. A curtain of dust filled the air, speckled on occasion when the pilot turned so the sun streamed into the windows. He could smell "nulomoline" a colloquialism for the grease used in weapons as well as the acrid-sweet stench of fuel. Other than an occasional shuddering when hitting an air pocket the flight was comfortable.

"Hey Marine," Mike spoke to the young sergeant who had loaded his gear on board, He was stocky with a large chest pushing its way out of his green skivvy shirt with his hair buzz cut, ready for action. "What do you know about Guam that might help me?"

"Well Sir it's the largest in the Micronesia group. I read, Sir, that it's 30 miles long and was formed by two volcanoes. The island itself is actually the peak of a submerged mountain that is over 37,000 feet above the Marianna's Trench. You'll recognize it when we get close 'cause it looks like a giant footprint." Mike detected a slight twang when he spoke; maybe Iowa.

"That's interesting," said Mike, "That means it's over five miles high. We got the island from Spain in 1898 and the Japs' occupied it in 1941 and about 40 percent of the Guamanian people are Chamorros, descendants of the island's original inhabitants and other Micronesian islanders. There are also some Filipinos, Spaniards and of course Japanese mixed in there. I know that 'Hafa Adai' means "Greetings from Guam" and that the word Guam in Chamorro means, "We have", Mike continued. 'Many of them still believe that a brother and sister began the world. When he died she used his eyes for the sun, his eyebrows for rainbows and other affectations of that sort. When she died she became a large promontory rock. The Jesuit priests that came with the Spaniards saw to it the islanders converted to Catholicism.

"We'll be looking for Mount Lamlam Sir. It's over 1,300 feet high. The pilot will bring us in over the western shoreline from the Philippine Sea side. Some days you can see the Cormoran and the Takai Maru subs where they were sunk."

"Wasn't the Takai Maru sunk by the submarine Flying Fish?" asked Mike.

"Yes sir," replied the young man his eyes sparkling with pride, "Weighs over 8,300 tons." Mike felt the aircraft veer to the right as the pilot turned north. "That's Lamlam on the left there sir. He's gonna follow the coastline over Merizo, Umata Bay, Agat and Tumalaglago. Better suit up sir," he cautioned. Mike buckled on his chute after he positioned his throwing knife just below the back of his neck, his combat tomahawk on his belt to the rear, and his K-bar combat knife on his web belt with ammo clip for the '45 he would carry. There would be no M1 rifle on this campaign. Checking his pockets he found Atabrine to ward off Malaria and halogen tablets for water purification, a handkerchief and toilet paper. He was ready to go. Standing by the open doorway his face took on a set of resolution, the camouflage paint making his face appear like that of death. When the young sergeant looked at him he spoke out loud "*TEUFELHUNDE.*" It's what the Germans called the Marines when they came up against them in World War One, it means Devil Dog." Mike began checking his equipment again. When he jumped he would carry his pack that had a bedroll with shelter half and blanket. There was also a poncho, which he would probably discard.

"I see you've laced a dog tag through each shoe lace on your boots. Is that so they don't rattle?" the young Marine asked.

"You guessed it," Mike responded. "You should also notice I have put a sock around my canteen so that it won't make noise when I remove it. Approximately 20 miles South of Agana, the capitol, he jumped hoping his parachute wouldn't be spotted. Intelligence felt this would be the place to start looking for the plane. Drifting slowly downward he was able to see that he was headed for a large stand of Yoga palm trees. Their white flowers stood out in the limited light of the dawn. He could always eat their marble sized blue fruit if he got hungry. Odors of death and rotting vegetation floated up to him. He crashed into the Yogas' tearing branches as he plummeted downward. Hanging about five feet from the ground he pulled his K-Bar and slashed the harness, which dropped him the rest of the way. "Jesus Christ," he muttered quietly, "That went well," no broken bones portended a successful mission. He kept his eye out for the brown tree snake, which though not poisonous could give a painful bite. He had been told that during a heavy wind storm thousands of these snakes went flying through the air like brown spaghetti.

Checking his gear he found a heading on the compass and set out for a ridge he knew to be to the South. He looked for a path he could use that would parallel it with as little noise as possible. He also looked for a Chamorro who was to meet him and be his guide. He had been told that this one was Manmakahnas or "ancient healer." The Spaniards, after killing 150,000 in 1672 dubbed them Suruhanos and Surhanas. He knew also the people worshipped their ancestors called "Aniti."

Spotting a path of sorts ahead he began to parallel it so as not to leave footprints; his guide was nowhere to be seen. Stopping periodically he would sniff the air for the telltale odor of Japanese cigarette smoke. A placket of odor of human death assailed his nostrils. "Dam," he muttered wrinkling his nose, "I hope that's a Jap I smell." Just then he came upon something that looked like a dog with teats trailing on the ground and full of mange. It was feeding noisily on what was left of a corpse in a Japanese uniform. It looked up, growled, and then went back to feeding. He continued forward.

Avoiding the Sword Grass as it would telegraph his movements to anyone watching as well as cut his flesh he was startled by a loud grunting sound. He fell into a crouch and looking to his left he spotted a local Carabao, a water buffalo type of animal quite plentiful on the island. It looked at him and chewed contentedly with no apparent intent of using those long, curved horns. "Easy Boss," he muttered quietly and kept moving forward toward some Fadang Palms he had spotted. Standing in the middle of them he had a clear view of what was up ahead. He noticed something moving on a branch. It was a housing of Bagworms on one of the trees and they were busy as hell. Edible he thought but only in an emergency.

He found a ridge overlooking a village area about a half mile from his position and calculated it was the place he was looking for as explained to him by G2. His face covered with camouflage paint could barely be seen among the heavy foliage of the Wild Betel Palms. Below was the Asmafine River. He heard voices and adjusted the glasses to the left spotting a waterfall and four young boys playing in the water; he guessed their ages to be between twelve and eighteen. A noise behind him caused him to crouch and turn pulling his K-bar combat knife in one swift motion. It was only a feral pig rooting around that had less interest in him than he had in it. He went back to watching the boys.. One kid was actually walking up the wall of the waterfall. He learned later the chemicals in the water made it like sandpaper. Mike watched with interest feeling it was great to see kids enjoying themselves.

Adjusting his "Binocs" he got the area in focus when a Marine patrol of four men approached the village. The point man was a sergeant carrying a carbine. Behind him were two PFCs and behind them a private with a BAR. As they entered they were greeted by the young boys who, hearing them approach, ran to meet them yelling "Maolek, Maolek," which Mike knew meant 'Good, Good'. He was too far away to hear well but could make out a few words of Chamorro, the local dialect that drifted up on the light breeze. Two of the Marines checked out the huts. Another hunched down and took some rations out of his pack giving it to one of the boys. The tallest of the four rubbed the head of a boy affectionately. All the men gave the boys something from their packs. The men finally headed out of the village continuing their assignment. He was going to track them but something about the boys' action kept his attention. As he watched they pulled some items from behind a Banyan tree. 'What the hell' Mike uttered under his breath, 'The little bastards are armed, those are rifles."

His eyes glued to the scene his stomach went into spasms as he watched the kids shoot the four men in the back. Puffs of smoke could be seen then the loud reports could be heard. All four were brought down by the treachery. One Marine rolled over, obviously severely wounded, managing to sit up and raise his hands in surrender. Mike could hear the gleeful yell of the kid as he swung at the man with a machete severing his head partway. Another ran up and swung twice until the head left the body and rolled on the ground. Mike watched in horror as they began kicking his head like a ball yelling some sort of victory cheer. The third lad approached each of the other bodies and sunk his machete into each of their heads in a silent *coup'd'gras*. Mike could hear the wet "Chunk" of each blow. He vomited but looked up immediately. They dragged each body into the jungle to bury it in a shallow grave after they stripped off the clothes and took all valuables. His face took a set of cold hate that only retribution would thaw.

"These little sons-a-bitches are paid assassins," he said out loud as he clenched his fists in rage, "And I am going to send them to hell." He slouched dejectedly against a Fadang Palm trying to dispel the anger that raged through him; he had to think straight. Hacked mercilessly to death then buried. Kids, they were goddam kids. But they were also brutal murderers who pretended friendship only to slaughter. He was under direct orders to not let it be known he was here and to take no prisoners. That was it; they had to be dispensed with quietly as he was also under orders not to fire his weapon. Moving swiftly, staying low, he covered much of the ground in just a few minutes and was soon behind a Banyan tree watching them cavort for the last time.

Chattering like chimps the assassins strutted in parts of the uniforms and showed each of the pictures and wallets taken off the bodies as they headed back to the village. They were older than he thought and all well built. Mikes camouflaged face, closer now, stared out dispassionately at them. Some ancient rage welled up and filled him with a need for revenge, a longing to kill. He was preparing himself to send these little bastards to the reward they had so richly earned. Not wanting to break radio silence he had deposited his Hallicrafter B27C radio in the crook of a tree with everything else but his tomahawk and K-Bar; he couldn't risk gunfire. Just then the staccato prelude to one of the many quick storms the island was subject to announced a miniature monsoon.

As the rain soaked everything he saw the boys run out of the hut laughing. They began rubbing their arms and legs with something that Mike soon recognized as soap taken from the murdered Marines. Once lathered up they waited for the downpour to wash them off. Then, as quickly as it had begun, the rain stopped leaving them covered with soap film. 'Good for ya, ya little bastards,' Mike muttered. They filed into the hut to wipe themselves off. Mike waited patiently, without moving.

The tallest of the boys left the hut situating himself at the beginning of some foliage at the side of the hut and began to urinate. Mike moved forward slightly reaching up and behind his back slipping the tomahawk out of the strips that held it in place. He left the protection of the tree long enough to get his bearings and bring back his arm. As the young assassin turned a barely perceptible whoosh preceded the wet thwacking sound of the weapons blade entering the skull dropping him like a poled ox. He went down on his knees silently, then pitched forward. "Welcome to hell you little bastard," Mike uttered to himself. "Hold the door open." He waited and watched listening to the chatter coming from the hut.

Two of the boys came out chattering and headed towards a hill. Mike skirted around the area running parallel to their course until he got ahead of them. As they passed he stepped out and behind them. Sensing his presence they turned, both raising their machetes to strike. Mike had reached up behind his neck and pulled a knife that hung down from a chain from its scabbard. In one smooth action he threw it forward. Piercing the throat of one just below the windpipe it severed the larynx bringing him down silently. All he heard was a choking gurgle as he went to the ground. The second boy was striking at him with his machete, which Mike sidestepped. Pivoting he came up behind him, place his right forearm across his throat and pulled him into his chest. His left arm went upward so that his left hand was grasping his own right wrist. He affected a *Chugari* snapping the head forward to crush the windpipe and break the neck which he heard pop and his body sagged to deadweight which he let fall to the ground with a thud. Mike retrieved his knife then headed for the hut.

Directly across from the hut was a stand of banana trees. Positioning himself just to the side he began whistling softly. Nothing happened so he made it a little louder. The last killer, the biggest of them all, cautiously poked his head out to look around. He was about eighteen years of age, large, muscular and carrying a Marine K Bar combat knife taken from one of the Marines he had murdered He also wore a necklace of Dog Tags as an Apache might wear scalps and had a scarf wrapped around his head. Seeing nothing he came all the way out. Mike stepped into view startling him, his face took on the look of fear experienced by all who knew their actions had caught up with them and for a moment he just stood there staring at this face of vengeance. Mike waited.

His adversary began to move to his left, knife hand holding the weapon with the blade down waving it from left to right; he knew a little bit about what he was doing. Sweat trickled down his face as Mike stood his ground, watching his moves keeping his eye on the weapon. He was babbling something thrusting his tongue in and out like a snake testing the air for scent. Suddenly he lunged and as Mike feinted to the left his foot hit the root of a tree throwing him off balance. The man took advantage of this moving forward and slashing downward cutting a deep gash in Mike's left arm. Blood began to flow downward but Mike did not make a sound nor take his eyes of his man. They circled, watching each other for an opening until Mike feinted a strike to his adversaries left which, when he parried, opened up his right side to attack. Mike did a 360 and as he came around and brought his blade across the man's throat almost decapitating him. By the time the body hit the ground blood was pulsating out and he lay prostate in the throes of death.

Mike ripped off the sash he was wearing and bound up his arm. He knew he would have to head in the direction the Marines came from to find a first aid station. Insects were arriving in droves at the site of fresh blood. He removed the dog tags from around the neck of the dead man, collected his other weapons and took off. A short way up Mike turned and looked back. He could see swarms of bugs which would be followed by beetles and soon predator birds to pick the bodies clean. He fixed the coordinates in his mind so he could tell them where to find the buried bodies. Finding the plane would have to wait.

CONFESSIONAL

"Hey Mike" the words jolted him back to reality. Sitting on the back deck he had been going over everything he had encountered so far and had heard someone coming up the side walk; he looked over to see the face of Joe Morgan. He had met him about a year ago at the health club. Joe was slender, a little less than six feet tall and kept himself in good shape by working out and usually had a ready smile. Dressed in Chinos with blue tee top and bare feet in tan loafers he looked every bit the suburbanite. His chiseled face with a prominent nose recalled pictures Mike had seen of Geronimo, the Indian chief. He had been with a local police department for thirty years and rose to "Watch Commander; at times his demeanor gave a clue to his past vocation. He often worked out at the gym with his daughter who was in the Army.

"Mike," he began, "You once mentioned a rototiller you had that I could borrow. The wife wants me to put in a garden and I don't have one of those devices." His wife worked in the cafeteria at a hospital. Mike had met her once and she reminded him of a thermometer she was so thin. It was a fine spring day, with Crocus pushing their way out of the ground and Joe was looking up at the geese caterwauling above them in the blue sky telling each other where they were going. "You know Joe," Mike began, "I am of the opinion those geese were born here on my pond, flew south with their parents and now have come back to use it for the birth of their offspring.

"And just how do you figure they know exactly where this pond happens to be after so many months and from so far away?" Joe asked good-naturedly.

"I think they have a built-in Magnetometer, provided by nature that works on the earth's magnetic field. No doubt there is a servomechanism type of gland in their heads that notifies them when they reach the pre-programmed area imprinted into their memory when they were born. Perhaps when they launch from down south it is not unlike a missile preprogrammed to reach this location with all of the coordinates built in." They watched as a very large goose glided in low, pancaked on the pond's surface and braked with its wings to stop in the center. "I can't argue with you 'cause I just don't know and you do make a lot of sense. Excuse me I'm going in to use the John," and he disappeared through the back door. Just then another bird appeared out of the East; Mike could see it going into an approach. Looking every bit like a fighter plane it slid down and forward skimming the Alfalfa field as it approached the pond. It too pancaked in with a squawk of triumph.. Mike's thoughts vacated to the island of Guam....

The largest of the Marianas, Guam was 30 miles long and just 12 miles wide. A US possession since 1898 when it was taken from Spain, it had been captured by the Japanese in December of 1941 four days after the attack on Pearl Harbor. It was made a target because it was a logical staging area for the operations towards the Philippines, Taiwan and the Ryuku Islands. It had a deep water harbor at Apra, suitable for the largest ships and two airfields suitable for B-29 Superfortress bombers. The 3rd Marine Division had landed near Agana to the north of Morizo and the 1st Provisional Marine Brigade landed near Agat to the South. The 77th Infantry Division of the army lacked amphibious craft and had to wade ashore from the edge of the reef. Mike was flown in as he had expert knowledge on IFF. The "Identification Friend or Foe" system basically consisted of a transmitter that sent out a coded signal to the aircraft. On board the plane was a transponder which, if set properly by the pilot, automatically sent back a coded signal and turned on a green "ACCEPTED" light on the ground based display panel. If the light didn't go on they assumed the Japanese had commandeered a plane and were going to try to take out the communications tower and they were ordered to knock it out of the sky.

Mike watched a Corsair scream towards the beach looking for a "Handshake" and there was none. "God dam it," he bellowed, "God dam it." Sweat beads channeled down both cheeks as he picked up the battery phone. "Take him out," he yelled into the receiver, "Take the son-of-a-bitch out now!" The shore batteries roared to life sending up a curtain of lead that shredded the wings and set the engine on fire. Like an ammunition fire hose they poured a steam of ordinance directly into the front of the craft. The plane tilted sideways as it passed over Mike; he could see the pilot. jumping Jesus Christ, he yelled, "The poor bastard is one of ours. He's one of ours, I can see his face. Stand down" he screamed keying the mike frantically, "Stand down dam it!" It was too late, the craft careened into the jungle, the palm trees falling behind like pick-up sticks winding up in a fireball; anyone left would be a clinker. Mike sank to his knees his legs folding slowly under him like one of those scissor car lifts in service stations. He just sat there saying "God dam it, god dam it."

"Hey Mike, you look like you're a thousand miles away," said Joe coming out of the house. Mike shook back to reality. "Where do you keep the rototiller? What did you call it?"

"It's called the Mantis," responded Mike standing up, "And it does an excellent job on small gardens. First I bought one of the large ones partly because the ad showed a ninety-year-old man with liver spots the size of pancakes rototilling happily with one hand. When I got the dam thing it was heavy as hell, cumbersome to handle and hard to control. I was using it one day and it veered sideways and got away from me. By the time I got it under control I had taken out half the strawberry patch, two tomato plants and cut a swath through the raspberry bushes. I considered writing to the manufacturer of that beast and accusing them of using a twenty-year-old weightlifter in disguise. But that little Mantis will do the job and then some."

They talked in generalities when Mike was prompted to make a personal inquiry. He looked at Joe for a minute contemplating the intense eyes under those black eyebrows.. Today Joe was speaking in disconnected sentences, as would a man with a problem he didn't know how to approach. "Joe," he began, "You got something eating you, something you want to get off your chest or discuss with someone?"

"No" Joe jerked a little when he responded, "Nothing I can think of." He paused, lowered his gaze then muttered, "That ain't true, I got something that's been at me a long time and I better discuss it with someone 'cause it's getting to me. It has to do with my age and my sexuality."

Mike just nodded and sat down on one of the benches that ran along the sides of the deck. "I doubt you have anything unique Joe and it is probably something many of us have had to deal with. At our age whatever hasn't slid down around our ankles has fallen off. What used to get hard stays soft and what should be soft is now hard. It's like Shakespeare said, 'we have wasted time, now time wastes us.' What is it?"

Joe positioned himself across from him, looked right into his face and said, "Some years ago I experienced my first inability to have an erection. The wife and I kidded about it and it didn't trouble me again for a month or so. It began to happen more frequently and a few years later I had trouble having an orgasm. An Oncologist I went to once for a Prostate test called it "pulling the trigger" and told me not to worry about it because at my age it was common. I did notice it had a lot to do with the season, like spring or fall." He looked at Mike lacing his fingers together as if trying to decide whether or not to go on.

Mike said, "Hell Joe we all have those problems when we get older. Are you handling it OK now?"

"Well", began Joe again, "I found that to have a climax I had to squeeze my legs together real tight and that helped me "pull the trigger" but that isn't what is worrying me. What's worrying me now is the old joke about a man and wife are making love and suddenly he stops. She says 'What's the matter, can't you think of anyone else either?' The implication being that they are so used to each other that to enjoy sex they have to pretend they are with someone else like a neighbor or movie star."

"I know the meaning Joe", said Mike, "And it's something we all experience. "There have been times I've had to imagine I'm back with a former girlfriend. Like I said, it comes with age."

"Dam it Mike, let me finish," Joe flashed. Just as suddenly his anger subsided and he looked up at Mike almost pleadingly. "Hey, I'm sorry but it is so dam hard to say what I am having trouble with that your interrupting is throwing it into the impossible category. Now just listen please." Mike sat back, rested his right ankle up on his left knee, and interlaced his fingers behind his head to give his friend a message that he had his full attention.

Joe began again enrobed in a calm hysteria. "Once I conjured up an image of a little girl being naked and me doing sexual things to her when I wasn't getting anywhere. I don't know why I did it or where I got the idea, but it worked so every once in a while I have been using images of little girls in my fantasies; It scares me Mike! I always thought child molesters should be castrated and now here I am with these fantasies. And a couple of times I actually imagined Marge being made love to by another guy with me watching and it aroused me so I do that sometimes now. I got the idea from an article I read in a magazine about aberrant behavior so I tried it. It works! And this is during making love to my *wife*." His suffering was so apparent that had he been standing next to him, Mike would have put his arm around him.

"Me imagining sex with a child or watching someone else with my wife. Jesus Christ what the hell is going on with me? Those are things I would never do in a million years," he looked like he was close to panic. Mike leaned forward a little. "And the worst god dam thing is I have even imagined myself making oral love to another guy, no one in particular, but some guy and that also arouses me. Can you see the problem here Mike? Am I turning into a homosexual and a child molester?" Joe's shoulders had drooped, his face was ashen and his eyes looked like cesspools of despair. Joe rose up, turned to face him, and then said, "Jesus Mike, what the hell am I going to do?" He was a man being attacked from within.

"Joe," Mike began, "What you are experiencing would scare the hell out of anybody. For the first time in your life you are questioning your virility, your morals and your mental status; you've got your very soul under scrutiny. I can assure you that what you are experiencing is not all that unusual or abnormal; that a hell of a lot of men go through the same thing."

"Just how in hell can you be so sure?" Joe fired at him. "Just what makes you say it's normal? Here I am a man in my late sixties with sexual thoughts I not only have never had before, I've never even read of anyone else having them."

"I'm telling you Joe they aren't that unusual," Mike persisted. "All men go through them in one way or another.

Are you aware that married men masturbate more than single men?"

Joe looked at him with a glimmer of understanding in his eyes and said," I can believe that."

"Once a man is married," Mike continues, "he can go from being a Greek god to a god dam Greek in no time at all. When a couple is courting they are different and it is the difference that is exciting. Once they begin to pull together on the matrimonial rope and take on each other's personality traits they become alike. She emulates him in some ways and he copies some of her traits. They have to agree on the children and religion and before long are a lot like each other. It's as though you take two pieces of metal that are magnets and put the South Pole to the North Pole; they grab onto each other. Change them around putting like poles together and they push apart and then begins the game of "Take Away."

"Wait a minute Mike," Joe protested, "What has this got to do with my problem"?

"Hold your horses," Mike chided, "I'm getting there. Keep in mind it is complicated. When the game of "Take Away" is in full bloom the woman uses her ultimate weapon, the withholding of sex. They do it subtly of course and often aren't even aware they are doing it. They develop headaches, backaches, discharges, yeast infections and God knows what else. They do it in a way that says, 'OK you don't want to take me to plays then I don't want to play', but in a way the man cannot refute. "He comes home expecting lovemaking. At the dinner table she says, 'I have been working all day and am so dirty I smell, I've got to take shower right after dinner.' When she goes to bed without showering the message is clear. After all who wants to stick his face between a pair of thighs' that may smell bad? It's subtle but it works. After a while masturbation while looking at pictures or watching an X rated movie can become common."

"Dam if you aren't right Mike," Jack said rubbing his jaw and grinning. "Hell, she'll shower if she is going to the dentist but only wash up if we are going to bed to make love."

Joe was leaning back now more relaxed than at any other time. He studied Mike's face for a moment then said, "Are you telling me that you have had some of these thoughts? Are you saying that *you* have dallied in this Sodom and Gomorrah of a fantasyland? You?"

"We aren't talking about me Joe, it's you we have under discussion," parried Mike. "Are you aware that some of history's most famous warriors had sexual relations with other warriors? The Samurai were that way. There was no word or concept in the Roman language for homosexual or heterosexual. In Roman times you were expected to use your male slaves sexually. I assure you that all of us have thoughts just like you described in one way or another. The important thing is we don't act on them; we just use them to help us achieve erection and orgasm when our physiology and wives change on us."

"Jesus Christ," Mike, "Whoever or whatever designed us sure fouled up. I understand that at the time the male is losing his abilities the female is just coming into hers. She doesn't have to worry about getting pregnant so her desires zoom right when his abilities to perform begin to sag." Joe stood there introspective for a few minutes then said, "Well while it is true I only have these unacceptable fantasies once in a while they still are not what I feel a man should have," he mused.

"Dam it man you have no control over fantasies only how you respond to them," Mike responded a little irritated now. "When you are hot you sweat; when you are cold you shiver; when you have trouble getting it up you have fantasies; it is all taken over by nature which is dedicated to your well begin. So let go of this shit about you being a child molester or homosexual. You are a man, nothing more and the sooner you accept that the sooner life will unfurl for you. Marriage simply legitimizes lust."

Joe looked at him quizzically for a moment then said, "Dam if you aren't a piece of work my friend. I feel OK now."

Mike asked, "Joe, do you know where a guy might pick up wrinkled skin like from salt water?

"Sure," responded Joe without hesitation, "Down at the Shedd Aquarium," as he got into his car. Mike had turned to walk towards the house deep in thought as Joe took off for home.

AQUARIUM

Mike had logged on to get driving directions to the aquarium and was soon heading down I 90 towards Chicago. A clear sky with little traffic made 75 mph mandatory. They had long ago taken down the 55 speed limit signs on the Northwest Tollway. He noticed planes queued up at O'Hare airport as he drifted into the Kennedy tollbooth. Past the Marriott he was soon at the "Eden's Whirlpool" junction and on his way past the "Cubs Park" exit. Just past Ohio Street exit he entered "Hubbard's Cave" named for an early settler Gurdon Saltonstall Hubbard made up of surface streets. The famous Merchandise Mart stands on the south side of the street and the "Billy Goat Tavern" is located on the street where it intersects with lower Michigan Avenue.

Mike had never been to the Billy Goat Tavern, founded in 1934 by a Greek immigrant, Billy Sianis who bought it with a bounced check which he made good with the proceeds from the first week-end they were open. He was quite a promoter and when the 1944 Republican Convention came to Chicago he put up a sign that read, "NO REPUBLICANS ALLOWED." The place became packed with Republicans demanding to be served propelling it into a place that one must visit.

Before long he turned into the Eisenhower expressway cutoff, Congress street, and headed east. First under the post office then the Chicago Stock Exchange and he turned right on South Columbia, took it to the Wm. L Mc Fetridge Drive then slid east behind the Field Museum of Natural History to Solidarity Drive. Here he checked the parking meters that ran all the way up to the Adler Planetarium, which were all occupied, then pulled into the parking lot next to the museum paid $7.50" and walked to the entrance of the John Shedd aquarium.

The Aquarium was a gift to Chicago by John G. Shedd. It was opened in 1930 as one of the first inland aquariums in the world. In 1933 Chicago hosted its second world's fair. The Aquarium was located immediately north of the fairgrounds and therefore gained exposure to a large international crowd. Among the collections added during the fair was a Queens Island Lungfish known as "Granddad." In 1971 the Caribbean exhibit was opened with a 90,000 gallon tank reproducing the Caribbean coral reef. They added the Oceanarium in 1991 for white-sided dolphins and beluga whales. The newest exhibit, the Wild Reef, recreates a Philippine coral reef based on the Apo Island Marine reserve.

The Shedd is also noted for it architecture of classical Greek which matches the other structures of the campus. The central aquarium building is octagonal, fronted by Doric columns and a formal staircase and topped by a dome. Aquatic motifs are worked in at every opportunity; tortoise shells, dolphins, octopuses, waves, and even the Trident of Poseidon can be found all over the aquarium's exterior and interior.

It was an early crowd snaking its way through the web labyrinth to pay the fee. Some people came for just the exhibits others for that and the Beluga Whale show. Fathers with backpacks shepherded their active children; it was often like trying to control a bunch of kittens racing about. Mothers with babies in chest and back harnesses followed not far away. The high dome resonated with voices and the atmosphere was one of noisy anticipation. Mike was intrigued with one young man who seemed to scoot across the marble floor, stop and began to walk then would take off like a shot again. He figured the boy had little wheels in the heels of his shoes that acted like skates. "Cool" he thought wondering where he could buy a pair. The kid got around like a Jet as Mike watched him disappear into the crowd his ragged pant cuffs sweeping the floor as they ballooned over his shoes.

Mike chose a comfortable looking bench and sat down so as to appear as a tired parent while he scanned the area. To his left was the large tank, the one with shark and turtles in their never ending spirals, pausing occasionally to look out at the crowds then continue morosely on. He fixed on one of the Nurse sharks as it meandered about and watched its fin break through the water. It circled in abject disinterest in anything around it, not even as a food source. His mind cascaded backward in time and he was watching the ocean waves off Okinawa, sitting in a rubber Underwater Demolition Team boat, looking for signs of sharks.

They were just outside of Buckner Bay at 2:00 AM on the leeward side of Okinawa in the UDT boat Mike had managed to borrow from the Underwater Demolition Team . They had a mission to board a luxury yacht manned by the Japanese to retrieve a German decoding machine known as Enigma. A few weeks earlier Mike had been summoned to the GHQ tent and briefed on the Intel they had on this craft. England, using a code-breaking scheme called BOMBE was striving to break the Enigma code but hadn't yet been successful. The Krauts used a four-wheel mechanism called TRITON, we called it SHARK, that was a real brain teaser. The German general Rommel had a personal code known as CHAFFINCH. The Japanese code was called INDIGO, which we had broken with a system called MAGIC. At this time the Italian code, known as C38M was of no consequence. But the ENIGMA was a "must have" and the rumor was the Japs had one and were using it on this craft

Mike was suggested for the task when they found he was on Okinawa in Radio Intelligence with the 6th Joint Assault Force Reinforced. "I understand you are one "kick ass" Recon Marine with good planning abilities" began Colonel Jack Conry, the spokesman for General Geiger. His six foot, lean frame was draped over a foot locker turned on end. He didn't wait for a reply. "General Geiger has received Intel that the Japs have an Enigma machine. They bought it from the Germans using gold they had stolen from China. It seems the German High Command was rewarding its Generals fighting in Russia with promises of great tracts of land. When the war went against them this became impractical. To keep the loyalty of their generals they were giving them gold; thus the trade of the ENIGMA for gold came about. The German high command wasn't too concerned since Japan was an ally in the plan to rule the world." The Colonel stood, walked over to the tent opening, stared out for a moment then returned to stand directly in from of Mike.

"This where you might shine Marine," he said. "We've got about 20,000 Okinawa Home Guards *(Boeitai),* and near 750 male Okinawan middle-school students who were organized into *Tekketsu* ,"Blood and Iron for the Emperor" volunteer units keeping us from getting to Yonabaru. It's obviously a temporary condition but we need some action now for a particular task. "The Nips periodically take a cruiser out into Buckner Bay, shown as Nakagusuka Bay on your maps, just far enough so that they can send and receive signals from Japan. When we try to approach they scoot back to shore. Our "spooks" think they have an Enigma machine on board and President Roosevelt wants it, now. I want you to get it for me."

Mike had been briefed on the problem in transit and had a ready reply. "I'm told there is four of the enemy on the boat Sir. Give me three men and I can pull it off. They have probably ranged in on the craft with the shore batteries so we won't take guns. Any gun shots from our M1's would be recognized and they would blow the ship out of the water. I will need a UDT craft. We'll board them like pirates and grab the booty."

The Colonel smiled at the typical Marine Corps assuredness and asked, "So what would you take as weapons? I know you men are unparalleled in hand to hand but you need the odds on your side. They will have weapons, including Samurai swords."

"Their swords will be of no use in close quarters Colonel," Mike responded. "I would like to have some cutlasses like they used to use to board ships protected by "Leathernecks."

"You mean pirate weapons? Where in hell am I going to get cutlasses?," exploded the Colonel who up until this point was impressed with the possibility of a successful mission.

"I heard there is an Ordinance Major in Australia who got a shit load of cavalry swords that he doesn't know what to do with," said Mike "Just get me some of those swords sir, and I'll cut 'em down to size. They'll do just fine as cutlasses"

"OK, I'll see if I can get some sabers flown in so put the plan in motion" Conry responded, his interest peaked again.

Mike chose three Marines from the 21st Raider Battalion as the assault team. The swords arrived by plane two days later, one more day was spent grinding them down. Mike showed his men how to use them, and the "Go" signal was given.

Faces blackened they shoved off at 0200 hours on a peaceful China Sea. The air was warm with a slight odor of smoke from the burning ships on the leeward side of the island. Kamikaze planes had turned some of them into floating crematoriums. Mike sat astern using hand signals having previously advised the warriors that not only was the smoking lamp out but the verbal clamp was on as well. His face blackened he had pulled a black watch cap over his head and had the others do the same. Kowalski, called Big Ko was up front keeping watch for any sign of periscopes or floating debris. A big Polish guy weighing in at 220 pounds, Big Ko was no one to mess with. He once walked up a hill with a BAR in each hand during one fire fight and took out a machine gun nest with three rounds in him. Spider, Mickey Wilson, sat starboard with one paddle. He picked up his nick name when he nailed a huge spider to the tent floor with his K Bar from 20 feet away. Jammer, Jack Ruland was portside also with a paddle. He was an expert with the knife and jammed up enough Japanese to rate the company title for kills. Each man knew his job and relished the rush they felt executing the campaign. The air was thick with testosterone and the urge to fight.

There was little light, other than from the target boat. Progress was painfully slow as the two wooden oars, painted black, were small and had to be used quietly by dipping them straight down, pushing back, then pulling them straight up so as not to create noise. They bobbed forward as Mike studied the small waves that sculled them. Big Ko pointed to a fin circling, an ominous sign, but it went away and didn't return which didn't mean the predator wasn't still looking for a meal.

As they got closer, Japanese music and words drifted towards them, becoming louder as they progressed. They nudged quietly into the side of the boat. Mike pushed along the sides with his hands until they reached a ladder hanging down: the Japs were not expecting company. Laughter and music seeped over the side and slid out over the water. Mike pointed to Big Ko, then to his eyes, then back, indicating he wanted him to watch as they ascended. He was to make a clicking sound if he saw anything move. He started up the ladder and silent as death each man rose, slid over the side, and lay on the deck awaiting further orders; Big Ko joined them. Mike pointed to Spider and Jammer then aft and they began sliding to the rear. Pointing each index finger at a man then at the cabin with a surrounding motion he soon had them positioned around the gangway. Pointing to his ear, indicating he wanted them to listen, he flipped up one finger at a time indicating he wanted a count of voices. After a minute they all held up four fingers and Mike nodded silently in agreement. There were four Japs on board, all to be eliminated. He heard "*Yohshio Sake o kudasai,* one of the Japs was asking for Sake. Just as he and another Raider started towards the gangway someone's head appeared humming a Japanese tune. They hugged the deck as the soldier staggered to the railing, undid his pants, and proceeded to stream used Sake into the ocean.

Mike rose silently, positioned himself immediately behind the man, placing the sharpened point of his cutlass at the base of the skull. His hand went around and over the mouth at the same time pulling the head back into the point as he jabbed it forward. The spinal cord was severed and all commands to the brain disappeared, the body sagged silently into Mike who then eased him over the side and into the water. The body bobbed in the gentle wave pattern like a rag doll then jerked downward as the shark reacted to the blood and took his meal. 'That's one' Mike said quietly as he slid over the deck towards the gangway. As he did he heard one of the Japs ask, "*Nanji desu ka*"? and someone answering, "*Hachihi!*" 'It won't be long before it wont make any difference what time it is', thought Mike. He motioned for everyone to remain in place. Finally he heard what he was waiting for, *Yoshio wa doko desu?* Someone was asking about the man Yoshio who had come up to relieve himself. He motioned to the two Raiders hidden on either side of the opening to be ready. A wave lifted the boat gently then set it down again in the dark water

Soon another body lurched through the opening. Weaving, the soldier began squinting around the dark. Like a silent apparition out of hell Jammer came up behind him. His left arm went around the neck, clamping the throat like a vise to disable the voice box. His right arm then slid over the wrist of the right arm then back so his hand cupped the back of the head. A snap forward was all it took to crush the larynx and break the neck, a perfectly executed *Chugari*. They lowered his body to the deck. Mike held up two fingers indicating the two left. They waited, black faces intently focused on the gangway opening. Apparently there had been too much Sake that night as no one came up to check on the first two men. Mike had to make a decision.

A direct frontal attack could result in gunfire, alerting the shore batteries and that they didn't want, at least not until they had the machine and were on their way, then they could sink the dam thing. Pointing to the body Mike motioned to Spider who was about the same build as the dead man and indicated with his arms that he was to put on his clothes. Without questioning he stripped off his pants and shirt and donned those of the deceased including the peaked cap. Mike indicated he was to descend the stairway backward then attack with his saber. Laughter rose out of the opening as the Raider went down as ordered. When he turned Mike and the others dashed down behind him just as his cutlass sliced through the air at one of the Japanese soldiers. He missed his mark and the man grabbed for his weapon as Big Ko brought his K Bar blade down on his head. The weapon became lodged in the skull. As he attempted to dislodge it the remaining Jap plunged his knife into his back. Mike saw him twist backward, attempting to turn and grab his tormentor. Apparently an artery was hit as blood spurted out and the Marine dropped like a log to the deck. The last man had been carried backward against the bulkhead by the other raiders. As they fought his hand found a pull-down switch and a siren began blasting through the night air. Spider plunged his K Bar into the man's heart and the fight was over.

"Look for a package about the size of a milk case", Mike yelled, "we have to get the hell out of here." They began searching the area turning over cushions, opening small doors until they found what they were after under a tarpaulin in the corner. "Is this it?", Spider asked. Mike went over, stooped down and smiled. They had the treasure. Carrying it topside Mike got in the UDT just as the first shell hit the front of the craft allowing the sea to flood in. The Nips had obviously pre-registered the craft so they knew just what elevation to use. He took the case from the two raiders who were holding it for him. A second shell hit amidships; Mike saw an arm and head spiraling through the air now illuminated by the ensuing fire. His men were gone. Grabbing an oar he paddled furiously when a spotlight lit him up for targeting.

Back on shore Colonel Conry, seeing the activity with the spotlight contacted the USS Minotaur, an ARL15 sitting in the East China Sea. He explained the situation to its captain and in a few minutes shells were being lobbed over the island at the Buckner Bay beach. The Colonel kept relaying the progress of the shells while the shore battery was getting closer to the UDT with their shots. Suddenly the light went out, the result of a direct hit. Mike yelled "Way to go Swabbies, way to go," then got back to the task of rowing ashore.

The adventure prompted the Marines to dub him "Pirate". They even fashioned a large ring and eye patch for him to wear. They held a brief service for the missing Raiders then opened some captured Sake and drank to their ascendancy into Marine Corps Heaven. One of the men tripped and sloshed his drink on Mike.

A jet of water hit Mike's face and looking to his left he saw a young boy with a water gun aimed at him. The lad was in a shooting stance, both hands holding the gun, exactly like he had seen them do on television, laughing as he squirted Mike. His embarrassed mother grabbed him by the arm and admonished him loudly, at the same time apologizing to Mike. Spotting a young man with a volunteer badge on a blue jacket standing near the huge specimen tank he wandered over and began a conversation. "I take it you are a Docent," he said. Kids pressing against the glass to "ooh and aah" over the sharks and turtles swimming around jostled him. The man smiled and replied that he was indeed. He informed Mike that he worked one day a week as a volunteer.

"Just how big is that tank?" Mike inquired as his eyes swept the room looking for the man he wanted dead.

"It's 90,000 gallons of water and 12 feet deep in the center. Actually the sides slope in so it isn't quite as large as it seems. The Nurse sharks are the largest fish in the tank," he continued helpfully. "They are slow-moving fish that may grow to 14 feet long and live among reefs in shallow tropical and subtropical waters. Unlike most species of sharks, the nurse shark can pump water over its gills so it does not have to swim constantly and often lies motionless on the sea bottom. They eat bottom-dwelling fish, crabs, lobsters, sea urchins, and shrimp and have been known to attack people. They have a small mouth as you can see and suck the flesh of most of the fish they catch. Sometimes I stay over and watch the cleaning crew feed them.

"How is the temperature and Ph monitored?" Mike inquired, "And do they use pressure transducers and thermocouples?"

The young man's brow furrowed in confusion, "I don't know details like that," he said finally. "Everything is controlled in a room above the display that you get up to through that door," he said pointing to a small entryway in the side of the display.

"Do they ever let anyone up there?" Mike inquired. "My business is concerned with such things and I would like to see the controls."

"I suppose I could check for you," was the reply.

"That would be great" said Mike enthusiastically, "I'll wait here while you do."

"Sure," he said, "Let me check", and he disappeared through the door. Mike looked around spotting the Gift shop filled with brightly colored items guaranteed to float the currency out of any purse or wallet. He made a mental note to visit the area before leaving. His gaze swept past each entryway into the various exhibit areas as he slowly periscoped around the rotunda. He just missed seeing a man sweeping the floor about 50 feet ahead of him; the crowd kept surging in front of him. It was Marcos, his as yet unseen quarry at the moment ogling a teen-aged miss whose breasts were much too perky and skirt much too short. His tongue came out like a rattler testing the air as he watched the exaggerated swing of her bottom through the crowd. "Like to get me some 'a that, he muttered softly pushing his broom in her direction trying to keep her in view. He knew the rest rooms in the area and was not above following her into one should she enter. His mind never stopped to reason when he was in heat.

"They said it's alright for you to go up sir," Mike heard from behind him. Turning around he saw the young man holding the door open. "You can go up if you want," he repeated. Mike thanked him and ascended the stairs. As he got to the top he saw a glass partition looking into the water was directly ahead and to the rear three cabinets with a tape recorder, an oscilloscope and various Keithley filters and Harman Kardon amplifiers that seemed to be it. "Rather a Spartan set-up," he mused as a young lady approached him holding out her hand. "Hi, I'm Robin the assistant manager. I understand you are in the controls business and want to see what we do here."

"I am and I do" Mike replied, "I Hope you don't mind but I was curious as to how you control and feed all these creatures." The bright young woman gave him a thorough rundown on the operation including the feeding schedules. There was a chest-high wall and that was all he saw between an observer and the aquarium itself. One could fall in, he reasoned, although with some difficulty. He asked some questions about the monitoring system and the seeming lack of much in the way of control equipment. She explained that most of that was below, in a basement level, and not available to the general public. His eyes followed a large turtle circling the enclosure when they swept past, then returned, to a figure of a man sweeping the floor just beyond the glass.

Marcos had decided to lay low because of the heat of the murders and took Miggy up on his offer. He showed up at the aquarium and was hire as a janitor. Miggy had told him of the inquiry Mike had made and they concocted a plan to lure him into a place they could kill and rob him. Miggy had driven out Route 31 to Barnard Mill road which he took north to Keystone road. There they found a parking area on the south west edge of Glacial Park and had walked in to the bog area. They got into a heated argument about money Marcos owed Miggy and Marcos stabbed him with a needle then took off leaving the body where Mike found it. Marcos had befriended one of the Hispanic technicians and learned about the serum they collected from the jelly fish. He had stolen a syringe full of the liquid to use on Mike but stabbed Miggy with it when they argued.

"What is that raised platform for, the one that looks out over the water?" Mike asked keeping his eyes on the janitor.

"Oh that's the feeding ramp where we stand to put food into the water after closing," Robin replied. "By standing on it they can reach over the top of the glass and pour whatever their feeding into the tank."

As he stared the man turned and looked up, Mike stiffened, he was looking into the face he had seen in the video from the young woman's house, "Thank you," he said hurriedly as he headed down the stairs and out into the crowd. Turning right he walked quickly, eyes searching for the man he was going to kill.

Marcos had moved to the left side of the building preparing to move into the toilet area where he would mop the floor and watch the little boys. He had an affinity for young males and had approached more than one to engage him in conversation. He was always friendly but probing to see if there was a chance for a little "fooling-around" with the lads. He instinctively looked up. He caught sight of Mike across the room scanning the area. When their eyes met something in the way Mike reacted told Marcos he could be trouble. Dodging into the restroom he opened a door at the end of the sink area and disappeared down a narrow hallway, closing the door behind him just as Mike cautiously entered. Mike looked around, saw that each stall door was open and walked in front of each one peering inside. A look of consternation crossed his face as he knew dam well the man had come in here. Then he saw the door.

Pulling slowly it opened to reveal the pathway down which his target had vanished. It was no wider than 20 inches, lined with bare two-by-fours and illuminated by a single light bulb hanging down from the ceiling area. Entering he got the stench of moist wood. Apparently he was somewhere behind the main tank area. Edging cautiously forward he squinted to bring the darkened area into focus. It was a dank, dreary place to be and he wasn't at all at ease as he moved forward. Ahead there was a turn to the left at which point the wall recessed inward. Marcos had positioned himself in that recess with his straight razor poised to slice through Mike's neck when he showed himself. The blade gleamed in the dim light. Marcos relished the moment, a vile grin having taken a set on his face. Water would not be the only moisture on the floor this night. Mike stopped, peering ahead, sensing danger but shook his head and stepped into the target area.

As Mike's head started to come into view Marcos's arm muscle flexed preparing to sweep the razor downward. Just then a youthful voice cried out, "Hey mister, what's in here?"as a lad entered the corridor having seen Mike go through the door.

"Don't come in her son, it can be very dangerous," responded Mike and he retraced his steps. The young man backed up, sweeping curious friends behind him through the door as Mike exited and closed it behind him.

"Fuck," muttered Marcos, closing his weapon by dragging the back along his left underarm. Shoving the razor into its pouch just below the pant line in back he left his hiding place and proceeded further into the area to another, hardly perceptible door that opened out into the cafeteria. A cacophony of metallic sound from food trays being slid along rails poured into the passageway then was gone as the door closed.

Mike spent an hour trying to spot the man he was sure had killed his friend's daughter. When his search proved futile he decided to leave and return another day. Exiting into the afternoon sun he paid the attendant in the parking booth and took Mc Fetridge Drive to Columbus then to Congress and down the ramp and onto the Kennedy. He was formulating a plan even as he passed through Hubbard's Cave. That pimple on the ass of humanity was his and he would find a way to take him. In a half-hour he was at the tollbooth and onto I90 towards Rockford. As he approached Route 31 he realized he was hungry and decided to pull off for the Spring Hill Mall. Paying his 30 cents he proceeded to the mall area and pulled into the Olive Garden parking lot. Their salad bowl and Eggplant Parmesan had long been a favorite of his.

LITTLE GIRL GONE

He was seated immediately, placed his order, then sat back to look out the window into the parking lot of an Aldi's store just across Route 31. He sat contemplating his next move which would have to be soon, before his target moved on knowing he was being sought. An Asian couple came in with a little girl and was seated directly across from him. The daughter had the most beautiful almond shaped eyes, with an ebony hue that spoke of ancient beauties. She looked directly into his and smiled revealing brilliant white teeth in a frame of liquid alabaster skin. He returned her smile. Looking into her eyes his memory cogs turned backward, so far back...

It was a pleasant day; as pleasant as is possible when one is in combat on a distant island like Okinawa. The island was 67 miles long and from 2 to 16 miles wide; a small area in which 150,000 men would be killed. Mountains and jungle covered the northern part of the island. Mike was in the southern part which had low, rocky hills. Composed largely of coral rock filtering rainwater provided many caves which the Japanese used to their advantage. Mike had read that the islands were surrounded by the most abundant coral reefs in the world with rare blue corals found off Ishigaki and Miyako islands. Sea turtles returned yearly to the southern islands to lay their eggs although this will no doubt be changed with the carnage taking place this year. Some of the troops wading ashore were stung by poisonous jellyfish. The sugar cane, pineapple and papaya gardens were devastated by ordinance from the ships hove-to off shore.

There was a breeze off the East China Sea that brought a cooling effect: it also brought the odor of decaying flesh; human. This wasn't surprising, as there had been vicious fighting here the day before. In addition to the *Kamikaze* planes, Kaiten *(Heaven Shaker)* miniature submarines and *Ocra (Cherry Blossom)* one-man torpedoes, the American forces were faced with the 44th Japanese Independent Mixed Brigade. Fighting had been heavy. They had been embroiled in a battle at Kakazu Ridge, two hills with a connecting saddle. The Japanese had prepared well and fought tenaciously hiding in caves with machine guns and explosives. They would send the Okinawan civilians at gunpoint to get water and supplies for them inducing casualties in the thousands. When the rains came the hills became muddy and covered with spent ammunition and a soup of dead bodies. Often sliding downhill in the mud a Marine would find his pockets full of maggots.

Mike had sent his platoon ahead to take command of a small bridge while he checked out an odor of human death hanging in the air to see if it were American. You learn to tell the difference between animal and human death soon after encountering it on the islands; the human plackets of odor have sweetness to them. His combat boots kicked up tufts of dust that settled immediately on his pants as he proceeded towards a hill. As he rounded it he could see there were people lying on the ground.

Continuing forward he saw a woman, then a man and next to him a little boy, all lying in the dust. There was blood everywhere. It looked like a mortar round had hit their party as they fled. There were two suitcases spilled open nearby with clothing and some utensils scattered about. They looked like they had worked in the pottery kiln in Naha; the woman was wearing a bright blue kimono now saturated with blood; the man wore cotton pants and jacket; the little boy in short pants and T-shirt: the side of his head was missing. The large flies had arrived and were already depositing their eggs into all orifices. Mike stood there sorting out his feelings, trying to understand the insanity of war.

He heard a sound from behind and in one movement swung around with his M1 pulled off his shoulder, aiming in that direction. It was a little girl, she appeared to be about six years old, trying to sit up; she was bleeding and dazed and had apparently been laying there unconscious. She looked at him and smiled weakly. He ran to her, dropped his weapon as he fell to his knees, picked her up and cradled her in his arms. She rested her sweet little head against him. Mike looked around for a Corpsman, knowing full well there wasn't any help to be had, but he had to do something. He sat there cooing to her trying to think of something to sing. He began to instinctively rock back and forth.

This sweet angel of innocence looked up at him with beautiful almond shaped eyes that had an ebony hue to then. "Is my puppy alright?' her words, in English, broke through the quietness of this graveyard..

He looked down into her little cherubic upturned face. She had the smoothest, prettiest complexion he had ever seen. He choked as he wiped bloody spittle from one corner of her mouth. It was then he noticed the little body of a puppy she had fallen on and covered with her body. Its eyes were closed and it did not respond when he reached down with his left hand and stroked the smooth, light tan fur. Picking it up he placed it on top of her and positioned her hands over it. "Here's your puppy Honey, he's sleeping.

Her tiny hand began stroking the soft fur, she said weakly, "Sister says he needs lots of sleep 'cause he's so tiny little" her hand fell away as her arm slid down and hung loosely. They sat there, a Marine, a little girl and her puppy as a mild zephyr wafted over them. Mike began to sob quietly.

"If I die will I see Jesus right away?" she asked in a tiny voice that was fading. "Sister says that when we die and go to heaven we see Jesus right away." Her eyes closed, her head lay to the side.

"Now you aren't going to die," he wasn't aware of the tears streaming down his cheeks. He sat back clutching her tightly to hold in the life. He mustn't let it leave her body, he had to do something.

Her little head moved slightly on his chest as she continued weakly, "I hope I get my wings when I get to heaven, sister says... Her head began to droop now and then she was gone, into a sleep from which she could not be roused. A line from Shakespere's Henry IV came to him: *In thy faint slumbers I by thee have watch'd and heard thee murmur tales...*

He studied that sweet, innocent face. There he was, a tough combat Marine, sitting in the ancient dust of a remote island, holding a dead child, choked up with the insanity of it all. There was absolute stillness, as though the world, in shame over what it had done to this innocent angel, was as sad as he was. He looked around for anyone, anything that could be of help. He looked from face to face, from the mother, to the father to the little boy. He looked back down at the child he held, his face contorted with agony. This was not a situation he could brace with a bayonet or M1. This carnage gave true meaning to the insanity of war. "Sir," a voice called out...

"Sir here's your salad," the waitress said setting a large bowl in front of him jarring him back to the present. Picking up a breadstick he knew what he would have to do.

No Recidivism

Mike left at 3 o'clock calculating he would arrive in the loop about 4:30 PM. He figured that his quarry, being one of the janitors, would remain after closing to clean up the floors. Parking in the Grant underground parking garage he walked up to Michigan Avenue and hailed a cab. Arriving at the entrance to the Shedd he entered the main area and headed for the restroom with the door leading into the interior of the aquarium where he had chased the man before, being careful not to be seen. Settling just inside the doorway he waited for the place to close listening to a few people enter and leave the bathroom facilities as he stared at the bare two-by-fours, ignoring the damp smell of mold. He dozed more than once until finally he could hear no one entering the room on the other side of his hiding place. The luminescent hands of his watch told him it was 6 o'clock, the place had been officially closed for an hour.

Easing out from his hiding place into the toilet area he stopped and listened for voices, any sound that was human. Creatures still moved silently around in their tanks to the musical burbling of water pumps but now without an audience. Approaching the main tank he saw movement out of the corner of his eye. Looking up through the water he saw the man he was after standing on the feeding ramp getting ready to throw food to the fish. He headed towards the door he had used previously, entered and ascended the stairs staying to the sides of the treads to avoid any squeaking boards.

As he reached to top of the stairs he could see Marcos just ahead getting ready to dump food chunks into the water from a bucket. As Mike approached the bottom of the ramp he was standing on he seemed to sense his presence turning to look behind him. He saw Mike and his predatory instincts must have set off an alarm that this man, whom he saw before staring at him, was a threat. Dropping the bucket he reached behind his pack and pulled out his razor. The pieces of fish hit the ramp floor so that when he took a step forward to come off the ramp he slipped, lost his footing falling backward into the glass partition which broke with the force and weight of the impact. He yelled as jagged pieces of glass cut into his arms, falling into the water and sinking immediately. By this time Mike was on the platform and the man's head bobbed to the surface. He reached his hand up so Mike could take it and help him out. Mike just stood there silently watching the sharks respond to the blood in the water. Marcos screamed as one of them pulled him back down into the water while the other made a passing bite at his body. Thrashing his arms he raised up and yelled at Mike to please help him. Mike stood dispassionately watching nature take its course. One of the sharks had seemed to attach itself to the man's face as if to suck out his eyes as he took him back under. By now a large turtle had come to feed.

Mike got up on the platform so he could look down into the tank and watch the carnage. There was a feeding frenzy now with even smaller fish taking turns at biting into the body. Without a word Mike descended took the steps down and sought the delivery entrance which he found at the rear of the building. He left by a side door and began jogging toward the underground garage contemplating the other two faces he had seen on the tape.